DUSTRUNNER

BOOKS BY DEAN F. WILSON

THE CHILDREN OF TELM

The Call of Agon
The Road to Rebirth
The Chains of War

THE GREAT IRON WAR

Hopebreaker
Lifemaker
Skyshaker
Landquaker
Worldwaker
Hometaker

THE COILHUNTER CHRONICLES

Coilhunter
Rustkiller
Dustrunner

HIBERNIAN HOLLOWS

Hibernian Blood
Hibernian Charm

A COILHUNTER CHRONICLES NOVEL

DUSTRUNNER

DEAN F. WILSON

Cover illustration by Duy Phan

First Edition 2018

ISBN 978-1-909356-22-1

DIOSCURI PRESS

Published by Dioscuri Press
Dublin, Ireland

www.dioscuripress.com
enquiries@dioscuripress.com

Welcome to the Wild North

CONTENTS

Chapter

Chapter One

BLOOD FIND

You never did get used to it. The sight. The smell. The horror of it all. You told yourself it was normal, but there wasn't anything normal about it. Folk weren't supposed to die this way. Folk weren't supposed to be found this way. But that's how the Coilhunter found them.

When Nox stepped his thick, buckled boots down, they squelched in the blood. With so little moisture in the desert, that was a rare sound. Even now, the blood was drying quick. It wouldn't be long before it was just another red stain.

He surveyed the scene at Ilouayisca, casting his eyes across the rows of cone-shaped tents and huts. They were like an artificial mountain range, going off into the dusty haze. A blood-splattered mountain range. The animal skins that lined those dwellings had crimson handprints on them, and it wasn't the blood of animals.

Nox'd almost stumbled over the first body, a scrawny child lying face down in the dirt, with a bullet hole in the back of his head. He'd clearly ran for help, but there wasn't any. Whoever did this made sure of that.

The next body wasn't far behind, an old woman, who looked like she might've tried to shield the child. It didn't matter. The killer had bullets for the both of them. Hell, they might've had some to spare.

But when Nox passed between two of the tents, like the entrance to a valley of death, he found far more bodies than one man could leave behind—the Coilhunter included. There were dozens of them, mowed down as they ran. Most hadn't even had time to grab their weapons. The killer came in fast, took them off guard. Why, it must've been an army.

Nox tried to find a reason, a purpose for this heinous crime. They still had their belongings, they looked like a docile tribe, and you couldn't slave-drive the dead. Nox didn't like the thought that maybe there wasn't a reason, that maybe someone just did this for fun.

But this was the Wild North. This was the land of the lawless. Nox was the law.

Nox paused to squat down beside a woman and her two children, huddled together at the door of a hut. The mother's eyes were still open, as if she wanted to remember the killer in the afterlife. The sight of them reminded Nox too much of his own family, mercilessly slaughtered as well. He'd gotten the bad guys. That only helped a bit, but a bit was better than nothing. Nox promised he'd get whoever was behind this too. And you can sure bet that he kept his promises.

He stood up, just as the wind kicked up the dust around. He shielded his eyes with his cowboy hat, but he didn't have to shield his nose and mouth. The mask did that. He could feel the tank of chemicals and oxygen on his back firing into overdrive, filtering out all the impurities. It was a pity there wasn't something like that for the Wild North as a whole.

Then the dust settled, and Nox could see better than before. The tents went on, row by row, and between them were more bodies. This wasn't just a killing. This was a massacre. And a new question rose in Nox's mind as he saw all those smooth, dead faces: where were the men?

He heard the sudden sound of scree falling behind him, and turned fast, with his hand already reaching for his hip. It was a woman, far off, carrying a trembling pail of water on her shoulder. She was from the same tribe. She was the lucky one. Now, she was the only one.

She looked at Nox, with his dark blue coat stained with blood, with his dual pistols for making blood, and with his grim eyes for gunning down the innocent. He could read her mind on her sun-kissed face. To her, he was the killer. To her, she was next.

"Now, you wait a minute," he said, his voice as coarse as it always was, which didn't help. An involuntary plume of black smoke blasted out of the filter on the side of his mask, making him look even grimmer. Boy, that was something.

The woman took a step back. Her hair was dark, falling down her back in straight lines. Some tribes said your hair showed the path of your life, so you sure as hell didn't want any curls. She wore a tan-coloured apron with strings of beads hanging from it. No doubt there was a purpose for it, but right now all she could do was clutch it with the hand not holding the pail.

"I found 'em like this," Nox said.

But why should she believe him? Who was he to her, other than the man amidst the bloodbath? All those women and children were at the wrong place at the wrong time, but now, so was he.

Nox tried to reassure her with his eyes, but his cowboy hat made them even darker. "I'm here to find out who did it."

The woman ran, dropping the bucket of water. If anything, that told you it all. People paid a high price for that life-giving liquid, so rare in the desert. As Nox watched the woman run, and debated whether to run after her, he promised himself that whoever was behind this crime would pay a higher price.

Yet he couldn't help shake the feeling deep in his gut that he might have to pay it too.

Chapter Two

FUEL

Nox's instincts made him follow the woman, but that just made her run all the quicker. He hoped to explain himself, but he also hoped she might know who did this, if she was just willing to listen to him and maybe do some talking of her own.

"Stop," he urged, with that same level of grit in his throat that told you that if you didn't, he'd do it for you. He couldn't help but sound like that. That was who he was now, or who he'd become. The gentler side of him had died with his family.

But she didn't stop. You see, she couldn't help but be afraid. When the Coilhunter came for you, you ran.

Until there was nowhere else to run.

She skidded up to a steep drop, turning sharply. Her hair clattered in the breeze. You'd think the wind was trying to tie knots in it. She held the edge of her grey skirt to keep the wind from seizing it too, and maybe to stop her trembling fingers. She looked at him fiercely.

"Now, you just wait there," Nox said, as gently as he could—which wasn't gentle at all.

She waited, but only because the cliff behind her

made her wait. He could see it in her eyes, could see her mustering the courage, deciding just when to make the plunge. Even now, she was shuffling her feet back. It wasn't quite running, but she was still getting farther away from him.

"I'll find whoever did it," Nox said. "That's a promise."

Of course, she'd probably heard plenty of promises from the local gangs. Words were like the desert sand, plentiful and blowing here and there, never quite amounting to anything. Actions were rare, or at least the good ones were. They were buried beneath the sand.

"You stay back," the woman warned, holding out her index finger as if she could ward him off with it alone. That was mighty brave of her if she really thought she was facing whoever slaughtered that village. But then, what other choice did she have? When you faced death, you ought as well be brave.

"You got it," Nox said, another promise. "But maybe you can help me find who did it."

But she kept backing up, inch by inch, until even the wind felt brave enough to push her over.

"Wait!" Nox shouted.

But she kept going, stumbling over the edge.

He dashed forward and extended his right arm fast and sudden, which triggered the mechanism for the grapnel launcher strapped there. The hook fired out, straight down to where she fought with the breeze. She caught the edge of the hook with one flailing hand, almost tugging Nox over as well. His boots caught the edge, and he grabbed the wire.

When he looked down, he saw she was hanging by the tips of her fingers. The drop was far. No one would survive the fall.

"Hang on!" he cried, even as her fingers slipped.

And then the moment went from bad to worse, for all their shouts and cries drew something out from a small cave in the wall down below. They hadn't seen it in the flurry, but they soon saw the wolves that came out from their den. They were brown and grey, with red eyes that glistened in the sunlight, and yellow teeth that begged for a feast.

The woman saw them and screamed. If she fell, maybe the drop wouldn't even kill her quick enough before the wolves pounced. The dogs leapt at the cliff wall, snarling and howling, filling the ground below with their saliva. The faint yap of a wolf pup came from inside the den. It'd have a piece of her too.

Nox tried desperately to reach down, and she tried just as desperately to reach up, but their fingers didn't meet. She looked at him with eyes of a newfound terror. She wasn't afraid of him above. She was afraid of death below. That was the thing about death. It came from everywhere.

She dropped another foot, and both of them gasped. Nox felt the wire grinding against the fabric of his gloves, chaffing the skin beneath.

She slipped again, crying out as she dangled. No matter how much she inched down, there was still a tremendous drop to go, enough to kill or cripple her. Enough to finish off the tribe.

Nox's first thought was to do everything he could to save her. But he had another thought that tried to push and scramble over the first: that if she died, whoever was out there, whoever was watching, might blame him too. She was the only witness, and to some it might look like he had pushed her over. If the wolves even left anything of her to find.

He hated the thought, but self-preservation has a way of killing off the kinder thoughts of the mind. All that mattered in the end was that the woman lived. It didn't matter why.

But there she went, two feet now, her own hands tearing from the wire, which itself was torn and frayed. The wire burned, just like the sun and the sand. The heat got everywhere, even into your soul. Some said that meant something. Some said it was the prelude of the heat of Hell. Well, if Nox was going there, at least he'd be used to it.

"Don't you go!" Nox shouted down. He knew there was a time in a fall like this, when the muscles were starting to give way, that you'd decide to give up. After all, what had this woman left to live for? It was maybe only her own self-preservation that had her hanging on as tight as she did. Maybe in her mind, she wondered if she could just let go, and let go of the pain of the world as well. Nox never let go. The pain was another rope. You could cling to it to live, or you could wrap it around your neck as well.

But Nox didn't see the signs of giving up in this woman's eyes. He saw the fire, like he saw the fire in his own when he dared to glance in a mirror. The fire followed him everywhere, into his dreams and back again into the waking world. It made everything a nightmare—even him.

And here it was, burning strong in her eyes. It was the fire of vengeance, which could only be quenched by the kill. And yet, even then it cindered, burning away at you slowly, yet just as hot as ever. You could let it consume you, or you could let it fuel you.

So Nox did what he knew would work on him. He told her the horror stories. He threw diesel on the flames.

"Do it for them," he urged. "Do it for those who died."

And there it burned brighter in her eyes, and, deep behind, it burned hotter in her soul.

She pulled herself up, one foot, then two. She gritted her teeth and grunted through them, all to the sound of the howls below. Her eyes bulged with effort and anger. Her pace quickened, three feet, then four, and her newfound vigour restored some of the Coilhunter's own. He wasn't saving her. She was saving herself.

If there was anything stronger than self-preservation, it was vengeance. In a world where it was hard to live for yourself, sometimes you had to live for another. It didn't wholly matter if the other was dead, so long as you sent someone else to join them. There were no shortages of candidates for that.

So she reached the top of the cliff, just enough to stretch a bloodied hand to Nox.

Then the wire snapped.

Chapter Three

THE WOLVES BELOW

She fell. It didn't matter how quick Nox could draw, or how quick he could fire the second grappling hook from his left arm. She fell faster. She fell to the wolves below.

Nox didn't take a moment to think. He latched the hook of the second grapnel into the earth above and launched himself over the side. The wire unwound swiftly from his weight, sending him down to the biting beasts.

But he didn't wait till he got to the bottom to fight. He'd already drawn one of his pistols, and he'd already clipped the paw of the wolf nearest the woman's fallen body. She wasn't moving, and maybe she wasn't breathing either, but all that mattered for the moment was that she wasn't dog food.

The wolves turned to him, snarling, crouching back, ready to pounce.

He landed with a thud, but the sound was drowned out by the clap of gunfire. The first of the wolves that leapt fell dead at his feet. The second took a bullet, but its body lunged into Nox, knocking him back and casting the pistol from his hand. He stumbled, but he reached for the handle of the next.

Another wolf charged, and it was a matter of who was fastest. Lucky for Nox, he'd had plenty of practice, even if the wolfs he usually fought wore the clothes of men. The hound's body skidded across the ground towards him, its head still moving, its tongue lolling to the side. That was just like some men too. Nox ended it as he always did—with lead.

But three more wolves were sniffing around the woman's body. One nudged its nose against her shoulder, and Nox doubted it was trying to wake her up. He could already see the dust-covered bones littering the opening to the cave. Hunger was a terrible thing. It was almost as overwhelming as vengeance.

The wolves circled him, baring their teeth. Nox sent out a menacing plume of black smoke from the vent on the left side of his mask, startling one of them. It was then that he struck, casting a second pistol down his sleeve, catching it in time to take down two of the wolves together, and then the third a moment later. He rarely used two bullets for one head, but sometimes the moment calls for it. And some men beg for it too. Those were often the ones you let go with a warning, so they'd tell the rest of the pack.

The dust settled, and there were far too many bodies on the ground. It wasn't the tribal village, but it kind of looked like a massacre. That's what you got when you went up against the Coilhunter, but then that's also what you got when he wasn't around. If it wasn't him holding the gun, it'd be someone else. That's why Nox held on tight.

And that's why Nox didn't sheathe them immediately. He was fast on the draw, but you were quicker with the kill if you didn't have to draw at all. The dust might've settled, but Nox's nerves were still on edge. Even the tumbleweed didn't dare move then, in case it got shot.

He tapped the tip of his boot against the woman's leg. Her arm looked pretty busted, and the rest of her didn't look a whole lot better. She didn't budge. After all that, it was probably time to dig a grave. At least he could say he saved her from the wolves.

Then he heard the whimper of a pup inside the cave. Maybe it was wondering, now that things were silent, if its parents were coming back inside. Nox tried not to wonder, but the thoughts pushed through, like a conscience. You had to be careful with one of those. It was what separated you from the criminals, but it was also what'd get you killed. You couldn't be too kind to the wild, because the wild was hunting you too.

Then the pup sauntered out, shivering. Its little eyes, filled with curiosity like little Aaron's, stared at him. The wise men say that the eyes are the windows to the soul. Well, in the Wild North, you didn't want to see into a man's soul. That's why you brought a gun with you—so you could seal those eyes shut.

Nox pointed the pistol.

He told himself this was mercy. He'd told himself that before.

"No!" the woman cried from behind him. Her voice was weak, weaker than the pup's. She sat up slowly, nursing her broken arm. That fall should've killed her. The land had spared her. Nox already knew what that meant for the pup.

He lowered the gun.

"You should be dead," he said. He meant it for the both of them.

She looked at him with grim eyes, and he saw the wounded soul behind. It looked a lot like his own.

Her voice grew crisp. "There's still time for death."

Chapter Four

CAMP VENGEANCE

They trekked back up the plateau, and that little wolf pup followed them, gnawing at the laces of Nox's boot. He had to carry his new female comrade for much of the way, and the sun took advantage of the fact, beating down harder and harsher, knowing it could take down two for one.

But Nox found some shade in the night, which came quick enough, and the three of them huddled around a campfire. You could've called it Camp Vengeance, because all of them'd been wronged in some way, but he didn't like to think of that, least of all when he was the one who'd wronged the pup.

"Probably should've asked earlier," Nox said, "but have you got a name?" He hadn't asked earlier for a reason. It was easier to bury the nameless.

The woman spit out a piece of rope she was using to tie a brace around her broken arm. Nox'd offered to do it, but she refused. Maybe she thought he'd done enough to make it broken in the first place.

"Umna-amma-dina," she said.

Nox worked on repairing his grappling hooks. "That's a mouthful."

"It is my name."

"I shortened mine."

"Why?"

"To make it more like gunfire."

"You mean, to hide yourself."

Nox grumbled, slotting one grapnel back into the launcher. "That too."

"What was it before?"

"Nathaniel Osley Xander."

"A mouthful," Umna said, though she didn't smile.

Nox smirked, though she didn't see it. "People keep findin' new things to call me."

"Curses," Umna suggested. "We have them for you also."

"Not what I meant ... but those too."

They paused for a moment in the awkward silence. It was there that you could almost hear the screams of the dead. That's why you occupied yourself with things to do, with books—if you could read—and pastimes. Nox'd used to make toys in his spare time, back when things were simpler, when there were little worries and bigger joys. He hadn't quite realised how big those joys were at the time. Of course, he still made toys—dangerous ones—but you didn't want to play with those.

"We're gonna have to go back there, you know," he said, finding his thoughts drifting back to Ilouayisca. Those folk deserved a proper burial, though he wasn't quite sure what the custom was for the Tiandala tribe. Those traditions varied starkly, and what you thought was respectful for one tribe might be offensive to another. Nox still had the pinpricks of darts and arrows as his learning-mark for that.

"I know," Umna said. She counted pebbles from one hand to another, like some kind of broken prayer beads. Nox wondered if they were meant to be broken.

"It ain't gonna be pretty."

She didn't respond.

"I'll find 'em, whoever did this," the Coilhunter swore.

"No," she said. "*We* will find them. That is the way now."

Umna fed the pup from her hand. It'd warmed to her quick. It gave Nox a squeaky growl whenever he looked at it. That was pretty much how everyone greeted him. Well, either a squeak or a growl.

"He likes you, huh," Nox said.

"We are bound now," she replied. "It is the way of the land."

"You lot have too many ways." Nox wrapped the wire of the second grapnel over itself, doubling it up for extra strength.

"It is better than the one way your people have … of killing everyone."

"I'm makin' a new way."

She paused and reached out for him, grabbing his arm. "Us," she said. "We are bound now too." She went back to feeding the pup, not even glancing up at Nox. "It is the way of the land also."

Chapter Five

PEBBLES

They travelled back to the village, half-hesitant and half-eager. They say the passage of time helps heal all wounds, but that's only partly true, and it requires a lot of time to do it—the kind of time most folk in the Wild North never got.

The bodies were still there, a little riper than before. The sun didn't give you much time to dig a grave. As far as it was concerned, the whole damn desert was it. The stench made Umna tie her neckerchief up over her mouth. Nox was glad he had his mask.

"What'll we do with 'em?" he asked.

Umna was already answering that by placing one pebble on top of each body. Nox hadn't noticed the markings on the pebbles before, and didn't want to ask. The wise men might've disagreed, but there was such a thing as knowing too much. Sometimes it was better—or at least easier—to be ignorant. If you were going to Hell anyway, why, it was better not to know.

"Do we bury them?" Nox asked.

"No," she said. "This is their village after."

"I don't follow."

"We build our village in the place we hope to live

and die."

"Right."

"The land provides now and after."

"You mean, this is your afterlife too?"

"Yes," she said, petting the head of the wolf pup, who hung out of her pocket. It couldn't help but salivate at the sight of the dead. "And we provide to the land also, even our bodies."

"So, that's it? You just leave 'em here?"

"No, I give them the blessing to move on." She placed another pebble. By now, she was running out. She hadn't enough of them for everyone. No doubt the village never thought they'd all be going together.

"Is that enough?" he wondered.

"Yes. To us."

Nox said no more on the subject. He wasn't sure how he wanted to go, though he knew his pebble'd probably be made out of lead. He didn't have a tribe to bury him, or to place a stone on his chest. Would he just be left for the sun? He glanced at it now, that taunting orb, just waiting for his day to come.

Nox looked for clues amongst the bodies, but there wasn't much to go by. They all died to gunfire, that was for sure, but with so many guns in the Wild North, that could've been anyone. Yet not many had the might to take down so many folk so quickly. It had to be someone good with a gun. Someone like him.

"I'm not findin' much," Nox said, careful not to disturb the dead. He wasn't so careful with the criminals. You had to earn that kind of respect. If you didn't deserve it in life, then chances were you didn't deserve it in death either. Nox'd heard tell of a belief amongst the tribes that the worst of men are just as bad after they die, that they still wander the land somewhere. Nox didn't like that thought. There was enough bad there already. But if it came to it, he'd hunt them too.

"They covered their tracks well," Umna said, rubbing her hands in the dirt. She sounded remote, like Nox. She was burying her feelings well, putting them aside for her people. "This must've taken much planning."

And it was true, but what was the plan? This village didn't have much by the way of valuables, not by the standards of most criminals anyway. They had some gold trinkets, but that was worthless nowadays. It was iron you wanted, and only if you knew a good coiner. There were a few of those in the Wild North, but the Iron Empire had the highest bounties on them, almost as high as Resistance targets. You didn't mess with the currency of the Iron Empire and not expect a reprisal. There was a reason those criminals hid in the Wild North. There was nowhere else for them to hide.

"I will need to come back," Umna said. "Only pebbles from the riverbed can be used here. The closest river is many miles north of here."

"Your speech is good," Nox observed. "What were you before all this?"

"A guide," she said. "For people like you."

"You mean, the lost," Nox mused. See, you could pretend you knew what you were doing and where you were going, but when you were hunting others you were just following their path. It was something else entirely to find your own.

"What were you?" Umna asked. She wiped her hands on her apron.

Nox took a long time to answer. "A toymaker. A mechanic." He sighed. "A family man."

"And that is gone?"

Nox took another moment. "I put a pebble on it."

Chapter Six

CRIMSON CLUES

Umna went through most of the village, stepping over bodies, counting the ones she hadn't seen to with her pebbles. It was a long trek to the river, long enough for the sandstorms to come and hide whatever evidence there was in the village, or to give those people a burial after all.

"What about findin' the killer?" Nox asked.

"I will find them."

"But they've already gotten a head start."

"The land will show me."

"You know I can't go with you," Nox said.

"I understand."

"I need to start this hunt right now." See, Nox didn't believe the land would show him much, except maybe a few more bodies. If anything, the land would make it hard for him. After all, it was the ally of the sun.

"I will find you," she said. She seemed pretty certain of it. Maybe she hadn't quite abandoned her old job. Maybe she'd be a guide to herself.

"I'll save 'em for you," Nox promised. "If I find 'em first."

She nodded to him solemnly. It was clear from

her eyes that she didn't like to admit that she wanted that, that she savoured the kill just as much as he did. When you looked to vengeance, it took over you quick. It became your blood. Your heart beat for the kill.

Nox kept looking for clues as Umna kept counting, and the last he saw of her was her back as she walked off towards the river. There wasn't a lot of water in the Wild North, and Nox wondered if there were enough pebbles on the riverbed for everyone there. She'd have a hard time carrying them all back in one go.

Twilight set in, taking the heat off the Coilhunter's back, but the darkness didn't help his search. He felt his stomach growl like that little wolf pup, but the sight of the bodies turned him off food real good. That was one way to deal with hunger in the desert. Another way was, well, to die.

He was about to give up and call it a night when his boot kicked off something in the ground. He fired up his lighter and crouched down, holding the light to the object. It looked like a small chicken wing, with the meat eaten clean off the bone. Now, you'd find those in plenty of places, but Nox knew at least one thing about the Tiandala tribe: they didn't eat meat.

This was the first real clue, but it wasn't much of a start. For all Nox knew, one of the prairie dogs could've dragged that in. But then, why didn't they drag some of the bodies out as well? Nox was full of a dozen questions, tumbling over each other in his mind.

Then he heard the click of a gun behind him.

Chapter Seven

IRON AND LEAD

Nox tried to reach for his pistol, but a voice stopped him.

"Keep those fingers off yer hips, now." It was a man's voice, rough and familiar. But that could've been anyone. Nox cycled through the Wanted posters in his mind.

"Come out o' the dark or go through with hittin' that trigger," Nox said. "I guarantee you it won't end well for ya."

"Now, now, Nathaniel," the man said, coming into the light. "You ain't in any position to be issuin' guarantees."

It was Sour-faced Saul, with that ugly mug you just couldn't help but want to slap. He was clean-shaven, though many thought he might've done himself a favour by growing a big old rug across his jaw. Now, he didn't like that name he'd been given, and you didn't call him it if you wanted to be friends.

"Sour-faced Saul," Nox said, stressing the syllables.

"Oh, boy, you're just askin' for it, aren't ya?" Saul replied. "We oughta put a cavesson on you, Nathaniel, if we don't put some bullets in you first." It didn't take much to rile him up. You could give him today's milk and it would've already spoiled. He wasn't a bad man, as men in the Wild North go, and wasn't the worst of the bounty hunters, but that wasn't saying a lot. The best of a bad bunch wasn't a medal you wore proudly.

But Sour-faced Saul wasn't alone. Iron Ike stood in the shadows behind him, a clockwork construct who'd taken to hunting bounties. No one quite knew why, and some thought he might've been secretly working for the Clockwork Commune. He had the shape of a man, which many constructs didn't, and he wore an old cowboy getup, which'd long been shredded in the hunt for past bounties, showing the dark metal limbs beneath. Combine that with his beady red eyes and you had something almost frightening. Almost as much as the Coilhunter himself.

"What's with the gun?" Nox asked Saul. He didn't bother asking Ike, because Ike kept his shotgun on you whether you deserved it or not. Maybe being a machine made him think he was exempt from the unwritten codes of the gunslingers. Well, being a machine didn't exempt him from the unwritten laws the Coilhunter enforced. He'd already proven that to the Commune.

Saul kept his gun low, and he played with the hammer. "It's what you use when you've caught someone in the act, Nathaniel. You should know that."

Nox glowered at him. "What's this about?"

"Oh, lookee who's sour-faced now. Are you seriously tryin' to pretend you're not standin' in a field o' bodies?"

"This is how I found 'em."

Saul cackled. "You crack me up, Nathaniel. Go on an' use another one o' those lines. Hell, I've got a list o' them from the lockup. Shucks, the Crimson Killer said the Devil made 'im do it." His eyes grew grim. "Did the Devil make you do it too?"

"Hear me out—"

"Like *you* do that," Saul scoffed. He tossed his head, flicking his blonde fringe out of his eyes. He did it often enough that he should've been called Whipneck Saul. It was just a pity for him that the other name suited him so much.

"I didn't kill these people," Nox swore.

Saul kept the pistol on Nox, but took several paces to the left. He grabbed a body by the hair and hauled it up. It was the only man in the entire village, and Nox hadn't spotted him before. He hadn't gotten to that side of the village yet. By the looks of the pebble-less bodies, neither had Umna.

"Now, Nathaniel, don't you tell me that ain't Bootlace Willett."

"Okay," Nox said. "I won't."

"See?" Saul said to Iron Ike. "He good as well admits it."

"I didn't say that," Nox crooned. "I didn't kill Willett."

"Now, is that so?" Saul asked. "What's that you got in your pocket there, hmm?"

Nox glanced down to the poster peeping out of his coat pocket. You rarely saw him without one. So why should that rolled-up paper matter? Because it had Bootlace Willett's face and name on it, and that juicy reward beneath. If there'd been a judge, it would've looked like a hopeless case. But there were no judges in the Wild North. Just executioners.

"I was huntin' Willett, but I didn't get to him in time."

"Looks like you got to him in plenty." Saul let Willett's body slump forward, showing the bullet hole in the back of his head. "Looks like you tore up the whole village to get to him."

"Well, I didn't. This was someone else."

"And I suppose it was someone else who carved your name into all those bodies along the road up the mountain?"

Nox couldn't even answer that. He hadn't even been up the mountain.

Saul scoffed. "You're a law unto yourself, y'are. Tell me, Nathaniel, how come you don't apply those same laws to yourself? It's high time someone brought you in."

"I ain't goin' nowhere," Nox said.

"You're gonna have to, willingly or by the rope."

The black smoke burst from Nox's mask. "I hope you brought your yarn."

"Oh, I cannot *wait* to haul your ass back to the Booth and get me some actual."

"Why wait?" Nox asked. "Why not get your iron now?" Nox had his two shooting irons primed and ready. They always were, even when he was sleeping. And right now he'd been caught as if he'd been counting z's. That's why you trained to kill in your dreams as well, because you never knew when you'd need to reach for your holsters.

Saul hesitated. It was why he hadn't already taken the shot. He'd survived all these years not so much by skill as by wisdom. He knew firing at the Coilhunter was almost like firing at yourself. Maybe he thought Nox would come quietly. Maybe he thought the presence of Iron Ike would help. He wouldn't, and it didn't.

Nox didn't budge and didn't blink. He took in everything and made his silent calculations: how quick he could draw, how fast he could duck and roll, and whether Saul or Ike would fire first. By rights, Nox should've already put a bullet between Saul's sour eyes. But you didn't kill the best of a bad bunch without becoming the worst of the batch. They said Nox was an unlawful killer. He couldn't now prove them right.

So Nox waited for Saul to muster the courage.

It was too bad for him that Iron Ike didn't need to at all.

Chapter Eight

THE BATTLE AMONG
THE BODIES

Iron Ike let loose the first blast, firing his shotgun. Nox barely had time to dive out of that machine's firing arc, and no sooner did he hit the ground than Ike hit the trigger again. Nox rolled, instinctively casting up four smoke canisters from his belt, adding to the cloud of gunpowder.

Sour-faced Saul wasn't far behind, firing from the hip like he always did. He never did raise that gun much higher, and Nox knew that was because he had an unsteady hand. It was knowledge the Coilhunter hoped to use to his advantage.

As they fired into the smoke cloud, Nox hopped over bodies as carefully as he could, letting the gunfire mask his steps. He thought maybe he could just run on out of there and avoid the gunfight entirely. But he thought wrong.

Nox had to dive again to avoid the next round of gunfire, and he couldn't help but tumble into the body of a woman, knocking the pebble off her chest. Nox prepared to dash away, but stopped. He rolled back, picking up the pebble and placing it back delicately on the body. Maybe these two bounty hunters were going to bury him tonight, but that didn't mean they had to disturb the rest of the graveyard.

He sprang to his feet again, zig-zagging across the field of corpses, trying not to become one of his own. Time and time again, he evaded those shots. But the hunter always has the better odds. They only need to catch you once.

Saul sent a shot that clipped Nox's mask, knocking one of the tubes out. The change in oxygen levels immediately made the Coilhunter gasp. He stumbled forward, lucky it hadn't clipped his brain instead. He fired two warning shots back at Saul, just glancing back enough to make sure they didn't hit too close. It was an odd thing shooting to miss.

But it didn't deter Saul. If anything, it emboldened him. They say there ain't nothing more dangerous than a man with a gun. Well, there ain't nothing more dangerous than a gunslinger who thinks he's lucky. Saul's sour face was growing mighty determined, and he showed it with his stride. He walked right through the smog, firing as he went, stepping over bodies like they were cracks in the earth.

Another shot pinged off Nox's steel-plated guitar on his back, adding another dent to the ones it'd earned before. It was pocked so bad that only a few more hits'd make it level again. But it still played a mean tune. It twanged intuitively as Nox dashed between the tents.

That was when Iron Ike clanged forward, blasting through the first tent and making a hole in the second. He was all construct, which at one time Nox thought might make him better than a man. It meant he followed the law to the letter. The problem was: who made the law? So long as Nox's name was on the list, Ike would keep on shooting. Nox needed to give him a reason to stop.

The Coilhunter stayed low, hiding amongst the bodies on the ground. Now, he didn't do a great job at it, but the night became a sudden ally. He knew why the criminals preferred it so much. He caught his breath, shoving the tube back into his mask. At this rate, he thought he might die before they even got their kill.

So he stayed low and stayed very quiet.

Saul sauntered up to the last tent, pointing his gun through the hole Ike had carved. Ike stayed back, watchful.

"Come out, Nathaniel," Saul jeered. He clicked the hammer. Some'd call it luck that spared him so far. Others'd call it the Coilhunter's mercy.

It was then that Nox flicked open another canister from his belt, unleashing a dozen mechanical butterflies. They fluttered through the opening in the tent, making straight for Saul, whose face couldn't curdle any quicker. Saul unloaded his gun, taking down three of the critters, but the rest of them broke through, spraying green gas into his eyes.

Saul faltered with a cry. He landed on his back, and he tried to swat away the butterflies with his pistol. That only made them come for him more. See, they sensed movement, and they were lured by it. It was why Nox stayed perfectly still. It was why Ike's motionless form didn't draw them either.

Saul conked out, laying down like the women and

children of the Tiandala tribe. But this wasn't his life after. He'd get to wake up and live another day. He'd know that Nox had been kind to him, and maybe he'd realise that this couldn't have been the same person who slaughtered these folk. Or maybe none of that mattered at all.

Right now, all that mattered was Iron Ike, taking careful, slow, methodical steps around the tent. A stray butterfly followed him, unleashing more of its toxic payload. But Ike didn't have lungs, not even the iron kind. He operated on clockwork, and currently he was wound up tight.

Nox prepared on the other side, hearing the grating of Ike's iron limbs. He could've tried to kill him, pull out that ticking heart, but Ike was good too, in his own way. Nox had learned that not all constructs were built the same. Maybe they weren't built bad. Maybe they learned it from men.

Ike came into view, and Nox barely spotted him before the construct fired. Nox dived through the hole in the tent, tumbling on the other side. His guitar strings made a little tune on the ground. Then Nox grabbed Saul's slumped body and hoisted him up to make a display out of him. He pointed a pistol at his head.

Ike stared through the hole in the tent. This time, he didn't shoot.

"Put it down or I put him down," Nox croaked. He made it sound like he meant it. He almost did. The few remaining butterflies sprayed their gas at Nox, but it couldn't penetrate his mask. Their colourful wings almost made them seem like a thing of beauty.

Deception was just another toy of the Coilhunter.

Now, Ike was a machine, so he wasn't used to reading people. He didn't get emotion like humans did. All he saw was a desperate man willing to do desperate things. And Saul was on the side of the law.

So Ike unclamped his hands from that shotgun, letting it bounce off his metal feet below.

"There," he said in his usual monotone voice. "I have complied."

Nox kept the gun at Saul's head. "You kick that far away."

Ike kicked the gun away, and it went farther than the Coilhunter expected. Ike didn't carry another. He was a monogun kind of machine.

"Now, I'm gonna take him with me," Nox said.

"That is a crime," Ike stated.

"Just far enough that you know to stay where you are."

"That is still a crime."

"That's where I'll leave 'im, and you two can go back to the Booth."

Ike tilted his head to the side. "Saul said we should not go back empty-handed."

"No," Nox said, dragging Saul away. "You go back with your lives."

Chapter Nine

A KILLER BY
ANY OTHER NAME

Nox dragged Saul out of the village, partly to shield himself, and partly so that that sour-faced fool wouldn't disrupt the dead. There'd already been a bit too much of that. Nox was better at making graves than fighting in them.

Iron Ike didn't follow him out. As promised, he stayed still, waiting for the Coilhunter to depart. Nox left Saul just outside the village. He'd wake up in an hour or two, groggy as hell, but still with two feet upon the earth. Nox only hoped that'd be the end of it, that Saul would call off this ridiculous chase. You see, in the Wild North, you could offer someone mercy, but that didn't mean you'd get any back.

Nox'd already tapped his wristpad, which sent his vehicle his way. It was a large monowheel, big enough to sit inside, with wide landship treads for desert travel. He hopped inside without even letting it come to a full halt. The box at the back was empty. Normally it had a body, a bounty. It looked like it was the Coilhunter who was going back empty-handed.

As he drove off, with his seat tilting to the side as he turned, he noticed that there were no footprints leading north to where the river was. Umna had covered her tracks well. He was glad. He didn't want Saul and Ike heading after her. She was better off without him. It was him they were after.

He wasn't sure where he was going, which made it seem like he might've been better off if she was still around. She was a guide for these parts after all. All he knew was that he had to get away, and hopefully pick up some clues elsewhere.

That was where the mountain came in.

See, you couldn't avoid that mountain, not if you were heading to or from Ilouayisca. It towered over that village like a silent guardian. Well, it must've been sleeping when the killer came.

A path led up the side, coiling around, growing narrower as it went. Nox followed it up. When he reached the highest path, he already spotted the bodies. They were hung up on racks, displayed like prized kills. Their clothing was torn, and on their chests were blood-laced marks. It was the men from the village—all of them. They came up here to fight. They came up here to die. What was strange was that it didn't even look like there was much of a struggle. It sure as hell wasn't a fair fight.

Nox stepped out of his monowheel, kicking the stand out. He left the diesel engine running. The exhaust pumped out black smoke to match the fumes from Nox's mask. The tribes often said you had to ride what matched your spirit. Well, that vehicle was fast and deadly. He left it running because he thought he might have to run soon as well. The headlights burned through the darkness.

He strolled up to the nearest body. An old man. Then the next, barely come of age. He wasn't sure which was worse, this or the slaughter below. There were no pebbles up here, just the harsh wind trying to flay the skin of Ilouayisca's men.

Then Nox spotted something else. Those markings on their chests. They weren't the wounds of the kill, as he first thought. No, those were letters carved into the flesh. They spelled out a name. They spelled NOX.

The Coilhunter held his breath. He moved to the next body, and the next, and they all had those same three letters. The blood was dry, but the wound to Nox's soul was fresh. In all his years policing the Wild North, no one had done this, not to him. The gangs had done unspeakable things to each other, but they feared him. Whoever did this had no fear.

Someone wanted him to fall. Well, this was all the push they needed.

Chapter Ten

ALL DOWNHILL FROM HERE

Nox worked through the darkness, taking down four dozen men, letting them rest. If where their bodies lay was where they'd be in the afterlife, it'd be cruel to leave them hanging. But this was the Wild North. You got used to cruel.

The night deepened, and Nox worried that Saul and Ike would follow him up the mountain. But then, he'd be crazy to go there, with no way out. He'd be crazy to go back to the scene of the crime. He wasn't crazy, and he was no criminal, so that's why he was there, doing God's work when he was napping. In the Wild North, the Devil never sleeps.

It didn't take long to get those men, young and old, down, but it took longer than it did to kill them. It was clear they'd been shot from above, from the very pinnacle of the mountain. They'd looked up to see their killer, and then their maker.

Nox climbed up the point of the mountain, holding onto the dusty vines. He found brushed-over footprints at the top, undisturbed by the sandstorms below. They were boot prints, probably male, but that didn't narrow things down by much. But at least they didn't look like the marks of the sandals or soft leather shoes that most of the natives used. This wasn't a war between tribes.

Then, as Nox ran his fingers through the dirt, he felt something: a bone. Why, it was another chicken bone, this one with bite marks. That was two of them, in both scenes of the crime. It looked like one of the killers was peckish. It seemed killing was hungry work.

He was just about to search for more when he heard a sudden noise: the far-off thrum of an engine. He ducked low and peered down the mountain. The veil of night covered it well, but he could see a faint light growing closer. Someone was coming, and it wouldn't do to find Nox with all those bodies. Sometimes doing good deeds can make you look bad.

He tried to climb down gently, but the rumble was growing very close, and he started to see his own hands from the glow of the light. He turned to see motorcycle drawing up, with three wheels in a row, and Iron Ike perched on top. Maybe they thought he was crazy after all.

"Halt," Ike commanded, reaching for his shotgun. If Nox had halted, he would've likely been picking shrapnel from his teeth.

So Nox didn't halt.

He leapt down, rolling past the gun blast. He threw himself into the seat of his monowheel and kicked away the stand. He pressed hard on the accelerator, and he zoomed past Ike, who turned his three wheels and followed fast.

It was all downhill from here.

Nox drove at full speed. He almost didn't need

fuel. Gravity did much of the work for him, and yet gravity wasn't enough. You see, you couldn't control that. You couldn't fill up your engine with it, couldn't make it burn for you. So he burned diesel like he was the sun, because Iron Ike was hot on his tail.

The night hid the path ahead, and the headlights revealed it a little at a time. At those speeds, you couldn't just rely on your hands. You needed your instincts as well. Nox clipped the edge of the path many times, and he was lucky he could turn that wheel quick or he'd have tumbled down the mountain, wheel and all. Ike couldn't turn quite as quick, but his bike was longer, so when one wheel rolled off the edge, the other two ground harder and pulled him back.

They spiralled down the mountain, with Ike taking pot shots at him. It was bad that it was Ike, because although he ran out of shells, he stored extras in his iron thumb, so he could reload with just one hand. Nox was counting the shots out of habit, waiting for the empty barrels, but it was a waste of time, because they didn't stay empty for long. One blast took one of the treads off the outer wheel of Nox's vehicle, sending it spinning down below. With enough shots like that, it wouldn't matter if Nox survived the descent. The monowheel'd sink into the sand below.

But that was the least of the Coilhunter's worries.

As he took another bend, he almost hit the breaks, because there was another three-wheeled motorcycle, parked horizontally across the road, blocking the way. Sour-faced Saul sat on top of it, aiming his pistol.

Now, maybe he thought Nox wouldn't crash into him, or maybe he thought he'd get a clean shot before the impact. Either way, he must've still thought he was lucky.

The Coilhunter didn't have much of a choice. He turned sharply, and the monowheel skidded sideways towards Saul's bike. That gave the bounty hunter a real good look at Nox, enough to make the perfect shot.

Except Nox wasn't just fast on the draw. He was fast with the drive as well. He booted on out of there, right over the edge of the cliff, leaving behind the biggest, blackest plume of smoke in his wake. Saul fired almost at the same time, but Nox'd already cleared the shot, and the bullet sailed by, right into Iron Ike, who came up fast behind. Ike tried to reach for the bullet in his plated head, but merely toppled to the ground.

Below, Nox and the monowheel fell. It was certain death, but less certain than the death above. As the air whooshed about him, he fired a grapnel up from the launcher on his right arm, wrapping the wire around the steering wheel. He fired the second one from his left arm, coiling the wire around his seat. Then he waited for the tug upwards as the wires unravelled and then went taut.

The pull was violent, almost throwing him off. The wheel bounced up and down like a child's spin-toy, but it was better than being a toy cast from the roof. Nox couldn't see too well below, so he had to yank one of the headlights to point down into the abyss.

It turned out the fall from there wasn't too bad.

At least not bad enough to kill you. The road had wound its way beneath him, and he'd bypassed the bounty hunters once again. He knew that wouldn't be for long.

He took out his pistol and fired up at both wires in quick succession, hardly even looking up to make the shot. The wires snapped and the monowheel fell with a clang. The parts groaned beneath him. It'd need repairs soon, if he didn't need them first.

He bounded off, just as he saw the faint glow of headlights coming behind him. He couldn't leap off the edge again. This time he had to follow the road, no matter what was in his way. So he put that boot down and almost prayed to the spirits of the machines.

But maybe he didn't pray hard enough.

The monowheel chugged forward. Steam rose from a vent on the back. Something clattered inside. The outer wheel jammed, then went, then caught again. He was barely moving at all.

The lights brightened behind him.

This was it. He'd have to stop and face them. He'd have to fight again, and this time he mightn't be able to spare a life. He'd be a real killer then. He'd have earned his face on the wall.

But one thing folk learned quick about the Coilhunter was that he never gave up. He was the Masked Menace, unwavering in his mission. If the wheel beneath him wasn't rolling, he'd walk the rest of the way instead. But he knew he wouldn't have to. He still had a few tricks up his blue cotton sleeves.

He jammed on the breaks, forcing the vehicle to a halt. Behind him, Sour-faced Saul must've felt like the stars had aligned for him. By most accounts, they had.

Then Nox tapped a button on the monowheel, which opened a little ramp at the back. Out of there waddled a toy duck, creaking as it went. It walked out onto the road and stopped, pointing its little beady eyes at the motorcycle coming its way.

Saul couldn't halt quick enough. He knew Nox well enough by now, and knew the rumour of his dangerous toys even more. He hammered the breaks and was almost chewing gravel.

The duck was waiting for him.

As Nox drove off, grinding at a snail's pace, the kind of pace that anyone could catch him, he took his shades from a panel in front and slipped them on. He heard that little mechanical friend of his give a loud quack behind him, followed by the brightest blast of light the night had ever seen. Nox didn't look back to see how Saul was doing. He could already hear him squirming on the ground, clutching his burning eyes. The light would fade, and the pain would dissipate, but by the time Sour-faced Saul could see again, the Coilhunter'd be gone.

Chapter Eleven

MUGSHOT

Nox drove for about a mile before the monowheel conked out completely. He patched it up as best he could, buying himself another couple of miles, just enough to head south-east to the Bounty Booth on the edge of the Wild North, touching Iron Empire territory. He knew he had to make sure they didn't put any official bounties on him. He had to get ahead of this, or someone might get his instead.

The monowheel just about fell apart by the time he reached the Bounty Booth. That hut was as defiant as he was, with its wooden walls standing against the sandstorms. It was operated by the Iron Empire, otherwise known as the Regime to its enemies. It was their only way of exerting control in this part of the world, where even the land rebelled against them.

Nox swung open the door. The hinges announced him angrily.

His eyes were immediately drawn to the posters on the wall. Normally he'd spot someone new to add to his list. *Dead or Alive*. This time he spotted his own ugly mug. The ink was still wet. The prize was far too high. One thousand coils. Yet, he'd upset enough folk that he knew some'd do it for free.

And there was Logan Hardwell behind the counter, looking a little more shaken than ever. Normally the Coilhunter was on his side. Now there was a criminal at the door.

Hardwell didn't say a thing, not with his mouth at least. His eyes said it all, those big, youthful eyes under his straw hat and black curls. He was an Iron Empire man, complete with the black uniform, and he looked odd behind the desk, never quite at ease. Now he had a real good reason for it.

Nox strolled inside, letting the door creak closed after him, cutting off the light. Just enough of it still got in to make his shadow long, long enough to reach Hardwell himself. They stared at each other, neither one blinking. They never did quite get along, but they tolerated each other. Now they wondered just how much of that tolerance was left.

"I'd say *'howdy, partner',*" Nox rasped, "but with that poster up, I wonder how much of a partner you are." He took a step forward, his boots making the floor creak.

"I don't want any trouble, Coilhunter."

"I don't either," Nox said, advancing across the room and snatching the poster down. It had NOX at the top, and underneath it was The Man with a Thousand Names. Now, he didn't quite have a thousand, but he was getting there. Each gang, each conman, each piece of desert scum, came up with a new one for him. That meant there were a lot of people who wanted him dead.

"You sure have a funny way of proving it," Hardwell said.

"I didn't kill those people."

"Tell it those that matter."

"I am," Nox said. "I'm tellin' you."

Hardwell was almost holding his breath. "I can't do anything about that. I … I've got my orders here." His hand instinctively reached for the Iron Empire symbol on his shoulder, a red cross over a black square.

"Well," Nox said, "you tell your superiors that this is my territory, and you don't go puttin' the sheriff's face up on the wall." He flicked the star-shaped badge on his chest, which he'd made himself, which had a different colour for each faction under his eternal watch. The Man with the Badge of Colours was another name they called him.

"You do if the sheriff's bad," Hardwell replied.

Nox's deep sigh sent out that familiar black smog. "Do I *look* bad?"

Hardwell's breaths were short and shallow. Maybe he thought he had to get the rest of his life's breathing done right here and now. "Someone saw you, Nox."

"Who?"

"I can't say."

"You *better* say."

"Now, don't you go threatening me, Coilhunter."

"I'm askin' nicely." And it was true. He usually asked with his gun.

"I haven't ever heard you ask nicely for anything," Hardwell said. "But I was sworn to secrecy on who saw you, in case you ever went after him."

"There's no 'in case'," Nox growled. "I'm goin' after 'im, with or without a name. And we go back, you and I. How many bad men did I bring in? Sure, didn't I get Ink Brannon when he was gunnin' for you? So, Hardwell, if you trust me, you'll give me a name."

"No one trusts you now, Coilhunter."

"This is a hive of criminals. Why'd I want their trust?"

"You'll need someone's. People are coming out of the woodwork to point fingers at you now. You made a lot of enemies here, some of them while you were out crossing off others."

"And you believe them over me?"

Hardwell sighed. "I don't know who to believe."

"Well, you give me a chance, and I'll prove I didn't kill those folk. Will you do that? Will you give me that chance I gave you when I took Brannon in?"

Hardwell rolled his eyes. He reached under the desk and produced a sepia photograph, which he placed down on the counter. Those things were rare in the Wild North, but it was even rarer to have one showing a criminal caught in the act. Except, it didn't show a criminal. It showed the Coilhunter. It showed him holding the body of a tribesman with his name carved into the chest, with a row of bodies pinned up behind him. Why, it looked like he was doing the pinning.

"I was takin' 'em down," Nox said.

"Maybe you were."

"I *was*."

"You've got to admit this looks bad."

"Well, you gotta admit that it ain't all about looks. What about the truth?"

"They say the camera doesn't lie."

Nox glared at him. "Well, this one's all smoke."

"I want to believe you, Coilhunter."

"Then believe me."

"But you wouldn't be the first good man to go bad."

"If I were bad, Hardwell, you probably wouldn't still be standin'."

Hardwell must've already thought of that, because he kept his other hand under the counter, where presumably he had a rifle cocked and ready. Not that it would've mattered. Hardwell should've known that by now. But he also should've known that Nox didn't kill anyone he didn't have to, or who didn't earn themselves a place on a poster.

"The name," Nox said, snatching up the photograph. He slipped it into his pocket where he used to put the Wanted posters. He didn't ever think he'd have his own face in there.

"You better not tell him I told you," Hardwell said.

Nox nodded. He knew he wouldn't have to. It'd be obvious. What Hardwell should've asked was that the Coilhunter make that man swear he wouldn't do anything to Hardwell in revenge.

"It was Honest Pete who had this."

Nox sighed. That didn't help his case at all. You see, everyone trusted Honest Pete, the good and the bad. If he told you he saw pigs fly, well then you'd get your airship and go hunting bacon.

Nox tipped his hat to Hardwell and turned to the door.

"You did this to yourself, Coilhunter," Hardwell said. If he knew what was good for him, he'd have kept his mouth shut. He was lucky it was Nox that heard him.

"No," Nox replied. "Someone else did. And I'm gonna find out who."

"Even if it kills you? Because it might. *They* might."

Nox glanced back from under his hat. "Not if I kill 'em first."

It was then that the Coilhunter noticed a few extra shadows stretching into the room from outside. Those could've been anyone, just another bounty hunter cashing in. Yet, if Nox were a betting man, he'd bet that bounty on his head that they were here for him.

Chapter Twelve

THREE GUNS WAITIN'

The Coilhunter had barely pushed open the creaking door before he was forced to dodge the first bullet. Outside, there were three other bounty hunters waiting. They didn't need a poster at all.

"Let me explain!" Nox cried.

But they kept on shooting. That was the trouble with explaining with words. If you explained with gunpowder, people listened.

As Nox rolled about, ducking and dodging, letting the steel-plated guitar on his back take a few of the hits, he started to recognise the men firing on him.

There was Dime-tossin' Dan, with his fabled modified pistol, which triggered a coin to flip from a crevice in the top every time it fired. A trick shot if ever there was one, back from the days when he robbed banks. It used to be a dime, from when the currency wasn't just flattened iron coils with the image of the Iron Emperor on it. He kept the name, and he kept his life. Nox knew that would change.

Beside him, crouching, was Jig Rivers, the thinnest, most limber bounty hunter the Wild North had ever seen. Some said he came from the circus outside Blackout, and his bright, multi-coloured getup supported that claim. He carried two tiny palm pistols, hidden in his fists, with just the tip of the barrel peeping out between his fingers. That way he could walk right up to you and fire, with you thinking he was unarmed. He was a gun-for-hire, and more often than not he was hired by the bad guys.

On the other side, perched behind some barrels, was Shotgun Samson, who strapped his shotgun shells to the top of his bald head. He was a former stagecoach protector, riding shotgun in the wild, right up until the time he started taking handouts to let those coaches get robbed. Now, he was claiming bounties on the same coach robbers who'd paid him. Talk about playing to win.

Together, they made up a posse known as Three Guns Waitin'. They were bounty hunters all right, but only between earning bounties on their own names. See, being bad paid, but there was good money on the good side too. Even better if you played both sides, because then you knew exactly who to catch.

It was no surprise they wanted Nox dead. They'd seen his busted-up vehicle outside. Maybe they thought he was the same. An easy kill.

They were wrong.

Now that Nox knew who his attackers were, and that they were bad, he had no quarrel with reaching for his gun. He slipped the guitar off his back, perching behind it for cover, and placed one pistol in the curve.

Dime-tossin' Dan was flipping dimes by the dozen, unloading everything he had. When he ran out, which didn't take long, he glanced at his pistol, which was just enough time for Nox to get in the killing shot. Dan stumbled backwards, tossing those dimes in the dirt, along with his blood.

Shotgun Samson was more sparing with his ammo, and Nox wasn't so sure his shielded guitar could hold up against those shells. He pressed a button hidden on the neck, which released a thick cloud of smoke. He knew Shotgun Samson wouldn't waste shots in the dark.

But Jig Rivers wasn't one to wait, and he wasn't one to hold back either. The Coilhunter had barely moved before he found Rivers somersaulting through the haze. That man could move, and he struck Nox in the jaw with the edge of his boot. It almost tore his mask off.

So, Nox answered with a fist, but Rivers dodged the blow, then brought his own fist in close to the Coilhunter's chest, with his palm pistol hidden inside. Nox turned quick, evading the blast, but Jig Rivers hopped right over him, using his shoulders for support. On the other side, he had another gun-filled fist ready to go.

Nox raised his own, but Jig Rivers struck him on the wrist, knocking the pistol from his hand. Nox reached for the second one on his belt, but Rivers flung his arm up and kicked him back, forcing him to the ground. Throughout this, Rivers smiled. He didn't even want the kill. He was just having fun.

It was a pity for him that hitting Nox's wrist triggered one of the buttons on the Coilhunter's wristpad. It set the creaking monowheel in motion, and that wheel rolled slowly towards its owner, and towards Jig Rivers in between. If it hadn't been so badly damaged, it might've bowled him over, but instead it acted as a distraction. Rivers slipped to the side, right into the path of Nox's bullet. Sometimes you got them by shooting one step ahead.

Jig Rivers dropped his pistols and felt the blood on his chest. It was quickly turning his multi-coloured shirt that one familiar colour. The look of surprise on his face was priceless. Why, you couldn't have picked a better mugshot. He toppled over without a hint of his former grace. You could dance through life, but most men died the same.

But Shotgun Samson was hoping to live, which was why he didn't waste his shots. As the Coilhunter gunned down Rivers, Samson hit the trigger. It was lucky for Nox that it was a shell of rock salt, because it might've cleaved his arm right off. Nox cried out from the pain of it, dropping his pistol. It was just as well he had some of his wits left, because Samson was ready for the next round, which Nox knew'd be lead.

Nox threw himself out of the blast, casting behind him a butterfly canister. But Samson gunned that canister down before they had a chance to hatch. He knew Nox's tricks—and he had some of his own.

Samson fired another shell just ahead of Nox's path, and this one had a blinding agent. It wasn't quite as bad as what Nox loaded in his toy duck, but it made your eyeballs itch and your aim poor. Nox tugged his hat down over his face to shield from most of the stinging substance, but some of it got through, turning his eyes bloodshot. He gasped at the pain, which just barely distracted from the agony in his left arm.

Nox stumbled forward, then dashed around the side of the Booth, trying hard to hold back a scream. He could barely close his left hand, and that didn't bode well for holding a gun. It was a good thing for him that he had two gun arms or he'd have been clutching sand six feet beneath.

Samson got up real slow on the other side, loading the next shell. Each of them made a slightly different sound, and this one clanged like lead. He pressed his back to the creaking walls of the Booth and followed it around slowly, turning that corner with his finger pressed hard against the trigger. That blast would've taken a man apart—if there was a man there to do it.

Samson must've heard a sound of his own then, because he looked up, spotting the Coilhunter on the roof. Nox fired right between Shotgun Samson's eyes, a little repayment for stinging his own. That crook spasmed on the spot, then dropped back into the sand, where his legs still twitched and his eyes still blinked erratically.

Nox hopped down with a grunt, tearing his neckerchief off to wrap tight around his arm. He ground his teeth together to stop himself from giving curses to the wind. That wind already carried enough of them.

Hardwell came out, his trembling hands clutching his rifle. "Hell!" he cried as he saw the bodies.

"They fired on me first," Nox said, boring his knuckles into his eyes. "You saw it."

"I didn't see anything."

"Well, you heard it."

"This isn't going to help your case."

"It's not supposed to. It's supposed to keep me alive." Nox tore the strap of shells from the top of Samson's skull and slipped them onto his belt. He took the shotgun too, strapping it to his back. If he was going to do this, he'd need all the guns he could carry.

"That won't matter now, Coilhunter," Hardwell said. "You're a wanted man. They're going to keep hunting you. I gave you your chance, but there aren't many who'll give you it too."

"I know," Nox said. "That's why I need to find who really did it. That's why I need to clear my name."

"Well, start in the Burg," Hardwell suggested. "That's where you'll find Honest Pete."

Chapter Thirteen

NO MUG TO SHOOT

The Burg was the capital of the Wild North, if there was such a thing. It was a city of sorts, built on a plateau in the middle of that wasteland, where all the dirt roads meet. If you needed something, chances are you'd get it there, though you'd get it at a premium. The Dust Barons ran that place like you had no other choice. Well, you didn't.

What was good about the Burg was what was bad about it for the Coilhunter. It was crowded. If you didn't want to be seen, you were a fool to go to the place of a thousand eyes. That's why Nox went in disguise.

The Coilhunter was a recognisable guy to most, what with having tapped his finger on many conmen's shoulders, and tapped his gun on others. That mask took some hiding, and the vat of oxygen on his back didn't help either. There were only so many hunchbacked men wandering the wilds.

So, Nox had to be creative.

He took what he could salvage from the mono-wheel and made himself an outfit like something the Dew Distributors would wear. See, those men were bulky, with big shoulder pads and armoured masks.

Best of all, they wore big tankers of water on their backs. They were the Dust Barons of that most precious liquid, giving you a drop for a month's wages. You couldn't argue with them or they'd just up the prices. They had whole factories of slaves toiling to make water, and make themselves even richer.

It was the perfect cover. Hell, it was the only one.

It took some time for Nox to make his suit, by which point he started to get some good feeling back into his left hand. He used the tools from his belt and the spares in the monowheel to carve up that vehicle and give himself a box-shaped cowl and box-shaped cover for his oxygen tank. By the end of it he looked all edges, like he'd stepped out of a world that hadn't heard of curves—like he'd stepped out of a dew factory.

He would've had to walk to the Burg, which wasn't at all in walking distance, were it not for the half-tread truck the Three Guns Waitin' parked outside the Booth. That beast guzzled fuel, and it wasn't anything like the monowheel for speed or control, but it worked. Right now that was all that mattered. The Coilhunter had a feeling he'd be thinking that a lot.

Normally he would've parked outside the city, where he wouldn't have to pay the Dust Baron tolls, but the good thing about looking like you were a Dew Distributor was that you got the perks that came with it. The Barons needed water just like everyone else, and they didn't dare charge their usual fees from anyone representing that powerful group. The tollman even got the door for him as he entered.

"Hot day out there," the tollman said.

"Is it ever not?" Nox replied.

He parked his new truck in one of the reserved areas, where no one batted a dry eye. People feared the Coilhunter, but people feared losing their water rations a whole lot more. You see, Nox might let you live. The desert wouldn't be so merciful.

"Pete," he said to the tollman. "Honest Pete. Ya seen 'im?"

"Oh, he'll be at his usual haunt."

That's all Nox needed to know. Some ghosts lingered at the site of the kill, but the best spirits were found behind the counter of the Jolly Gopher, where Two-glass Truman called the shots.

Chapter Fourteen

HONEST PETE

The Coilhunter swung those saloon doors in like he meant to gun down someone inside. It was part habit, but the other part was a genuine desire to do a little lead justice. He didn't have much left but a name, and you were bold indeed if you tried to sully a man with nothing else but a name. You might find him defending that to the death. You might find him pushing through the doors of where you sat slurping your prairie dew.

He strolled to the bar, noticing the averted glances. He was used to that by now, but they did it for another reason.

He found Honest Pete at the counter, with just a glass of liquid dynamite to perch him up. And there was Two-glass Truman behind the bar, lighting the fuse.

Nox sidled up beside Honest Pete, parking himself on one of the bar stools. He almost toppled from the weight of his gear.

"You," he said to the barman, trying to mask his voice. He probably didn't do a great job of it. "Fill 'er up." He slid an empty glass across the counter, just the one for him.

"Not got enough of yer own?" Two-glass said with a chuckle.

"This time I want my water with a bit o' colour in it."

"Right you are. Well, what's yer poison?"

"Whatever he's havin'," Nox said, nodding his head to Pete. "Looks like it's doin' 'im good."

Truman laughed. "Everythin' does Honest Pete good!"

"Well, whatever's your best medicine," Nox said.

"Here," the barman said, sliding two whiskeys over, "a pair o' overalls for ya."

That was how Two-glass Truman got his name. It didn't matter if you only ordered one. You were getting two, and you were paying for them as well. Most folk wouldn't have gotten away with it, but he was a Dust Baron. That meant you drank what he gave you, and you came up with the coils any which way you could.

"Pete, is it?" Nox asked that old sucker beside him.

Honest Pete was bobbing on his seat, smiling to himself. His wispy, white hair hadn't seen a comb in years, and it seemed his clothes hadn't seen a wash since then either. He was a drunk, but he was an honest one, and somehow always got on the good side of everyone. Now he was on the Coilhunter's bad side.

"Why, yessir!" Pete said, beaming. It didn't matter what you said to him—he heard it in good nature. It was something a lot of men could learn from, because it was hearing things in bad nature that often got you in trouble at the bar.

"What makes you honest?" Nox asked him.

Truman replied for him. "He ain't ever shot the crow, at least. More than can be said for the rest o' 'em." He pointed at one man in particular with his eyes. "You still owe me for a week ago Tuesday."

The man swatted his hand at him.

Truman's face flushed. "You do that again, Rex, and we'll have a word with this here Distributor and maybe you won't be drinkin' aught at all."

That did the trick. That man found coils in his pockets where he'd sworn there were none. Pete gargled the rest of his glass, oblivious.

Nox flicked a coil over to the barman. "Another one for honesty's sake."

"Mighty generous, sir" Pete said, as he slurped at the next drink. That's why he never got in trouble with Two-glass Truman. More often than not it was someone else buying the drinks.

"I heard tell you're good at stories," Nox said.

Pete nodded as he gulped.

"Well, hows about you tell me one now?"

"Oh, I heard a good'un lately," Pete said, swaying to the silent music in his head.

"What'd you hear?"

"Oh, boy, what didn't I?" Honest Pete said excitedly. "You see these ears? Why, my old pa said they were big enough to hear what goes on across the sea."

"Well, what'd you hear on *this* side o' the sea?"

"Well, I heard the Coilhunter's gone and cracked, so he did. Now, I never did think he was the crackin' type, but life's got its, hic, hammers." He gulped down another glass. "Calm me nerves," he said. Well, he must've had some nerves, given the empty glasses there.

"What'd he do?" Nox asked.

"Hmm?"

"This Coilhunter fellow. What'd he do?"

"Oh, killed him some savages, so they say. Now, I don't know if they're savages, I don't rightly know at all, but that's what they say. Never did, hic, make up my own mind on it myself." By the sounds of it, he never made up his mind about anything. That's why people liked him. He was a man of fluid opinion.

"Savages, huh?"

"Dozens of 'em. Up in Ilou—Iloua—up north."

"Now, why'd he do that?"

"For fun," the barman said. "Isn't that the way of those gunslingers?"

Nox bit his lip. "Not all of 'em."

"If you'd asked me a week ago," Pete said, "I woulda, hic, told you that this Coilhunter fellow, why, he ain't never hurt a fly. Now, a man?" He chuckled. "He hurt plenty of those."

It took some effort for Nox to hide his grumbles.

"Got me one of those Gosh-darn pictures, so I do," Honest Pete said. "Shows 'im in the act." He felt around his pockets for it. "Now, where'd I put it?"

Nox took it out of his own and put it on the counter in front of him. "You dropped it."

"I'll drop my own head if I ain't mindin'!" Pete held up the photograph. "Sure looks like 'im."

"Did you take it yourself?"

"No, no. I ain't got the money for that." He seemed to have the money for drink though.

"So, who did?"

"You're askin' a lot o' questions," Two-glass Truman noted. He polished his glass curiously.

"Well, we in the Dew Distributors like to know what's goin' on in the world. It affects our business." He glared at the man. "And you should know not to mess with the Distributors."

That silenced the barman for now, but it didn't change how he polished that glass.

"So, Pete," Nox said. "Who gave you this?"

"Why, I don't rightly know his name," Pete replied. "He was a short fella in a bowler hat. Kinda reminded me of Treasury type, truth be told."

"Truth be told, huh?" Nox said.

"He was a generous man," Pete continued. "Why, he bought me a top-shelf bottle, so he did. Was drinkin' it for days!"

"Well, a day," Two-glass corrected.

"Said he was lookin' out for folk. Wanted everyone to know how dangerous that Masked Menace was."

"Dangerous," Nox mused.

"A scapegrace if ever I knew one," the barman said.

"You knew 'im, huh?" Nox asked.

"Not personally."

"Guess that's why you're still alive."

The barman laughed. "Yeah, that and the good grog. You don't ever shoot a man who makes some mean scamper juice."

Nox held his glass up. "True, that."

"So," the barman said. "How d'ya drink in that thing?"

Nox eyed him coldly. "Through a straw." He stuck a tube from his mask into the whiskey and sucked it up noisily, like maybe he was sucking blood.

"You don't ever take off that helmet?"

"No."

"Don't it get hot in there?"

"It gets hot everywhere."

"Well, at least you got some water to cool ya down." Two-glass chuckled again. He was getting on Nox's nerves, but then maybe the Coilhunter was just rattled from this whole God-awful situation. He never had to hide before. He didn't like the feeling one bit.

Then things got a little worse.

Two-glass nodded to the door. "There'll be one o' you lot."

Nox didn't quite register what he meant. A gunslinger? A criminal? No. When he turned to look, he saw someone in Dew Distributor armour walking in. A real one.

Chapter Fifteen

DISHONEST NOX

The Dew Distributor swaggered to the bar. He could afford to swagger. He had the money other men had toiled to make. He sat on the other side of Honest Pete, three seats away. He'd been in such a hurry to get a drink that he hadn't spotted Nox yet.

That changed quick.

No sooner did he plonk his square behind on that stool than he leant forward and turned his head in the Coilhunter's direction. Nox tried to not look back, tried to stare at his drink, but he could feel the Distributor's eyes boring holes in his armour, exposing him.

"One for the road," the Distributor said to Two-glass.

"Sure, and one for you?" Two-glass quipped.

The Distributor didn't reply. Instead, he eased off his seat and took another one right next to Nox. He placed a heavy hand on his shoulder.

"What's this?" he asked.

"What's what?" Nox replied.

Two-glass slid two whiskeys towards the Distributor. The glasses skidded to a halt, untouched.

"What you're wearing," the Distributor said.

71

It took Nox a great effort not to let a puff of smoke out of his mask. "You should know."

"No, I *don't* know."

"Is there trouble here?" Two-glass asked.

Both Nox and the Distributor ignored him.

"This getup of yours," the Distributor said. "What's that all about?"

"The latest gear," Nox replied. "How long've you been away from the factory?"

The Distributor paused. "A while," he said hesitantly.

"Well, you oughta check in and get an upgrade."

The Distributor took his hand off Nox's shoulder. He was lucky he did, because another minute longer and Nox would've had to break it. The Distributor sat back down and tapped his fingers on his glass.

"Well, I'll be goin'," Nox said, standing up. "Duty calls." He took a few slow steps towards the door.

The Distributor gave him a nod, holding up his glass. "To the Great Distributor Above."

Nox instinctively moved his hand to his head to salute with his hat, but the helmet was there, hiding everything. It was then that the Distributor shoved open his own helmet and swamped down the whiskey, revealing everything.

Chapter Sixteen

DISTRIBUTED GUNFIRE

"You!" Two-glass Truman shouted, pointing a dirty finger at the Coilhunter.

Nox ran, or tried to run. That armour made him slower than even the set he'd used in the Rust Valley. He couldn't fight there, not with so many innocent people. He had to hobble out. He barely got to the door before the real Dew Distributor got up, reaching for his gun.

Now, here's something about the Dew Distributors. They'd fight anywhere, innocents or no. They were born fighting. The scarcity of water made it something worth fighting for.

So, that Dew Distributor had no issue letting loose three bullets towards the door. The first pinged off Nox's armour, which was a little tougher than the real thing. The second struck wood. The third took out a young barmaid passing by, who passed by for good.

Nox bounded through the door, almost taking it off the hinges. He raced out into the open streets, where the crowds of people turned in shock. You didn't start a gunfight in Dust Baron territory. Not unless you were the Dew Distributors.

And it was bad for Nox that there was a whole score of them outside the saloon as well. They turned to him, some making a move to chase, others making a move to kill.

Nox turned sharply and raced down one of the alleyways, zig-zagging his way through several more. He took the edge off some of the bricks with his armour and left a breadcrumb trail of shoulder marks across the walls. He wasn't running to hide. He was running to live.

But that armour was slowing him down, so he discarded parts of it as he ran. First came the helmet, which went like tumbleweed behind him. But he didn't throw it alone. He cast a smoke canister with it, and the first Dew Distributor coming his way tripped and became tumbleweed of his own. Nox did the same down every alley he travelled, throwing off one or two pieces in the smoke, a more deadly trail of metal crumbs.

Then, as he kicked off the shin guards, he leapt up a nearby crate and hopped across to another, before clearing the gap to the roof. It was a flat roof, like everything in the Burg, where the weather forced it to build wide instead of tall. It was the perfect place to run.

It was also the perfect place to follow.

It wasn't just the Dew Distributors now. It was the Dust Barons as well. Their guards came up fast, with no bulky armour to slow them down.

Nox jumped across to the next set of roofs. He tried to map his way back to the truck, but he'd lost his bearings in the sudden flight. Normally he went where the wind told him, but the wind was blowing against him now, just like everything else.

He approached the edge of another roof, where a Dust Baron guard climbed up straight ahead of him. Nox didn't slow or stop, and didn't even reach for his gun. He ran straight for the man, kicking him down and leaping over to the roof across the way. The guard fell with a crack that sounded bad. But it was better than the sound of gunfire.

Nox kept running, dodging bullets now and barely catching his breath. His feet hardly touched the roof of one building before he was back over on the other side. It reminded him a lot of the hunt for Handcart Sally. Boy, how things'd changed.

It could've been over if he were willing to fight. He could've laid waste to the Burg, and walked out alive. But then it'd be another massacre, just like at Ilouayisca, and he'd have done it for real this time. It was why he had to do it the hard way, the way that'd likely get him killed.

But the open rooftops of the Burg weren't a great place to run from gunfire. A bullet pierced him in the back of his right thigh. He almost fell, but he ran on through the pain. He could fall later. He could cry later. Hell, he could die then too.

But he knew he couldn't run for much longer, not here. He had to hide. He needed refuge, and the Burg wasn't the place to offer it. But there was nothing else out there, not for miles. So he'd have to make do with where he was. More than anything, he needed a friend. Well, he didn't have any of those, not here. So, then someone who wasn't entirely an enemy.

That'd be Harvey the Hound then.

Chapter Seventeen

ROOM IN THE KENNEL

Nox made his way to Harvey's den, tumbling in one of the higher windows, pulling a long silk curtain down in the process. The noise he made alerted Grapevine Bill, who came out of a nearby room with a trembling tray.

"You!" he cried, before dashing off down the corridor.

"Yeah," Nox groaned to himself. "You too."

The guards wouldn't enter through the window. Nox knew enough about the Dust Barons to know that. They had the kind of civility that came with cash. Harvey the Hound wasn't quite a Dust Baron, but he was getting close. He had most of the perks already: his own kennel and a dogbowl of power.

Nox followed the smell of rotten fish towards Harvey's room. He didn't take to the bone, not unless it'd been marinating in saltwater. You see, with water being so rare, fish were even rarer. You had to go far west or south to find the sea, and all the dangers that went with it. If you wanted fish in the Wild North, well, you better be swimming in coils.

Nox didn't knock. He knew Grapevine Bill had already announced him. That man was a sycophant

77

if ever he saw one, gathering his whispers for the Hound. Harvey knew all the best smuggling routes, not because he was good, but because Bill'd overheard the routes of other gunrunners.

The door creaked open. There was Harvey on his throne, with a big, black beard matted with the juices of the ocean's finest.

"Well, look what the cat dragged in?" he said.

Nox eyed him coldly. "You callin' me a mouse?"

"Well, you're not the cat. Not anymore." If he smiled any broader he would've swallowed the room. That dog sure loved being top of the food chain, though he couldn't quite wash the streets out of him.

"Last time we spoke," Harvey continued, "you were saying something about my face on a poster." He took one out of Nox. "Well, whaddya know?"

Nox hobbled in further.

"I should get this framed. You know," and Harvey smiled, "for old times' sake."

"Got myself in a bit of trouble," Nox said. He pawed at his blood-stained jeans.

"I'll say. More than you can chew."

"Well, life's already tough."

Harvey held his arms out wide. It'd take ten of him to touch those walls. "Not for me."

"I need a favour."

"You need a shelter," Harvey said. He smiled again. "Well, I've got room."

"I'm not stayin' here."

"Why not? Reminds you too much of how close I got to Taberah?"

"I don't care how close you got." He did though,

only because he didn't trust the Hound. But Taberah headed the amulet business, and she knew how to take care of herself. Why, she had a whole posse of people in the Resistance to take care of.

"Sure you do," Harvey said.

"It's not the place that gets me," Nox said, "it's the hidin'. I need to be out there, clearin' my name."

"*Uh-hoh*, it'll take some clearing."

"You have to believe I didn't do it."

"Oh, I believe you, Nox. It wouldn't suit you riding that high horse of yours if you were down here with the rest of us in the mud."

"Why don't you tell 'em that?"

"As if they'd believe me. Nox, they *want* to believe you did it. That way they get to bury you in the mud, name and all."

At that moment, there was a gentle tap on the door. That'd be Grapevine Bill. Yet there was also one hell of a commotion out there, and you didn't need a grapevine to hear it.

"You better hide," Harvey said.

Nox was already on it, firing a grappling hook up to the ceiling. He dangled there as four Dew Distributors marched in.

"Where is he?" one of them asked.

Harvey smiled. "Where's who?"

"The Coilhunter."

"Out hunting coils, I'd wager. Why, let's call it two waterskin rations."

"What's with the poster?"

"I was looking to make me some coils of my own. Quite a few for the Coilhunter's head, I see. Maybe we can share them."

"Search the place," the Dew Distributor said to his fellows.

"Nothing here but cobwebs and spiders."

"We'll see about that."

"Will you now? And you'll risk a war with the Barons for it, will you?"

"We'd win that war."

"Maybe you would, but that can't be good for business."

The Dew Distributor's face soured.

"Besides," Harvey said, "that'd only help the Coilhunter even more."

The Distributor said nothing. He gestured to the others and they left, with Grapevine Bill apologising profusely to them and commenting that he hoped it wouldn't affect their rations. It wouldn't, of course, because you only cut the rations of those who couldn't afford to fight for them.

Nox lowered himself down slowly.

"Well," he said. "Can you help me? For old times' sake."

Nostalgia must've been a powerful thing, because it made that dog tame.

"There's a smuggling route underneath the city," Harvey revealed. "I'll get you out."

"I owe you one," Nox said.

Harvey wrapped his arm around the Coilhunter. "Hey, things are good for me here. I think the world owes *you* a break. Come and rest the night, and let's see if we can't sway the world."

Chapter Eighteen

A WAY OUT

The night came and went like gunfire, leaving just the smoke of memory. Harvey got wasted on wine, Nox took out the bullet and recovered his strength, and they traded tales of bygones days in Taberah's company, when they were chasing ghosts. Well, it seemed like they were still doing that, because there was nothing left but spectres of those years.

The smuggling route under the Burg was long, but more than anything it was a place where no one looked your way—because they didn't want you looking theirs. People brought all sorts of things in and out of the Burg: women, amulets, waterskins. You weren't a city unless you had a constant flow of smugglers.

"Well," Harvey said, as he pushed a hatch door open to the land above. "This is it. Your freedom." He smiled. "And it was free."

Nox stepped out. He could see the Burg about half a mile to his left. He tipped his hat to the Hound. "Mighty kind o' you, Harvey, all things considered."

"Oh, I considered them all right," Harvey said. "You're just like me now, Nox. Welcome to the slums!"

He closed the hatch behind him. Two panels on

the sides lifted, dropping sand over the door.

Nox surveyed the land. It was empty for many miles, and he'd lost his transportation—twice. He didn't have enough supplies to make anything new, and he couldn't risk returning to the Burg to trade for something else. Everything else he had was in his workshop in the Canyon Crescent, which was many miles from there. He'd have to make the journey by foot.

He was glad he'd rested in Harvey's house, though his sleep hadn't been that restful. The walk to Canyon Crescent would take days. It wouldn't take that long for the sun to kill him. And that was if the people of the Wild North didn't get to him first.

He started out at dawn, following the unmarked trails, letting the sun cast him some shadows to follow. He muffled up through a sandstorm, losing his way for a bit, but there the sun was waiting for him on the other side, showing him the way again. But you were fool if you thought the sun was helping you. It was just showing the way to the grave.

The first day passed uneventful, which was something good, but his waterskins were already getting low. That heat half dried up the liquid in them before you got to take a sup yourself. That night, he killed a few small scorpions and fried their meat on a fire. At least they had some juices in them. It was a mild night, so he doused that fire as soon as he was done cooking. Campfire smoke was like a compass to a hunter.

He set out early the next day, while it was still dull. He got the feeling in his gut that someone'd caught up with him in the night. He didn't even pause for breakfast, because his gut stayed preoccupied with the sense of the hunt. The feeling didn't fade after two hours hiking through a cactus ridge, where he turned at the sight of a figure from the corner of his eye, only to find it was just another desert plant.

Yet another hour in, he halted. He knew for certain he was being watched. He scoured the area, searching every direction. It was all clear, with not a soul as far as the eye could see—and Nox'd trained his eye to see pretty far, to spot a snake in the sand. He breathed a heavy sigh of relief, but his gut kept telling him to move.

That was when she shot him.

Chapter Nineteen

THE LONG EYE OF THE LAW

The bullet struck him right in the gut. He bowled over, clutching the wound with one hand, holding his already-drawn pistol in the other. He scanned the area quickly, holding his gun aloft, but there was no one in sight, and there was no place you could pitch a rifle within range.

That could only mean one thing.

It was Long-eyed Lizzy.

He ducked behind a nearby cactus, just moments before the next bullet cruised past. He knew she could shoot from as far as 2,000 yards, and not just shoot, but kill. She had the gun for it, modified for maximum range, and she had the eye for it, modified as well. Even with his best rifle, he couldn't match her range. At best, he'd be shooting in the dark, and he never took a shot if he wasn't sure of the kill. Others'd done that before, killing the innocent. Nox'd rather die.

And he might still.

Long-eyed Lizzy blasted the top of that cactus right off, almost taking the Coilhunter's head as well. He dashed out into the open, finding new cover, but he knew he couldn't stay there, waiting to be brought in like a wild deer. And he sure as hell couldn't bring the fight to Lizzy, not without her mowing him down as he ran.

He threw every smoke canister he had left across the cactus field, making it look like a dust storm had been through. He tip-toed through the haze, keeping low. Then he took off his coat and wrapped it around one of the farthest cacti, and put his hat on another. That'd buy him some time.

He sneaked around the ridge, climbing the highest part of it and following it around through the desert brush, staying low as he went. He heard the rifle fire as he travelled, and he could tell that Long-eyed Lizzy was taking shots at scarecrows. See, you could see far, but that didn't mean your vision was perfect. Not when the Coilhunter was at work.

It took him a good long while to get close enough to fire his own. A good ten minutes in, he placed his pistol over the ridge. He shuffled up a few yards more until he could get a good look at his attacker. He needed to know for certain.

He found that woman perched at a boulder, ready to take the next shot. She was decked to the nines in her finest skirts, with that augmented eye of hers, helping her see farther, and shoot farther, than any sharpshooter ever did. She was one of the Deadmakers, the bounty hunter elite. They kept a score of their hits, and they even kept a score of the Coilhunter's. He was the one to beat. Well, you could beat him easier if he was dead.

"Liz," Nox shouted down.

She turned sharply. He fired, blasting that

mechanical eye apart. She screamed and grasped at the wires, dropping her rifle in the process.

He strolled down, keeping his pistol drawn. She backed away.

"Now, why'd you have to go firin' on me?" he asked.

"Why d'ya think?" she growled. Something about being made a little short-sighted didn't agree with her.

"Let me make you a proposal," Nox said. "You let me walk on outta here, and I'll let you do the same."

"You can walk to Hell!"

"Well, that's a long walk, Liz, and a lonely one. You know, you could join me."

She paused for a moment and considered her options. Most prey didn't give you a chance if they caught their hunter. The coin had *kill* on one side and *die* on the other. But sometimes, like when you met the Coilhunter, it landed on the edge.

"Go," she said. She wouldn't be much use without her good eye, and she didn't have so much courage at shorter range.

But Nox wasn't leaving much to chance. He took her favourite rifle with him.

"A little keepsake," he said. "You gave me one bullet, so I might as well have 'em all."

She tried to object, but stopped herself. She was lucky that was all he took.

Yet, as he strolled away, seeming like the old Coilhunter that went about the Wild North doing a little good, he knew he could only survive so much of this before someone got to take him out for good.

Chapter Twenty

ROAMING OASIS

Nox used one of his tools to pull out the bullet, biting on the handle of one of his pistols as he did. If you looked closely, you'd have seen a lot of bite marks there. He emptied half his whiskey canister onto the wound, and took a gulp of his own. Then he cauterised the wound, cleaning his good knife with some of the remaining alcohol and heating it up something terrible with his lighter. Boy, it didn't feel good, that's for sure, but dying didn't feel great either.

He continued on by foot for several miles, until the day wore on, and he wore out with it. The blood loss didn't help. The searing sun didn't either. He felt like every step required the effort of two, and it was quickly becoming three. He could feel his entire weight, and this other weight he didn't know he'd been carrying. His eyes blurred. The desert seemed to go on forever. It did.

"You'll make it," he lied to himself, because he wasn't sure of that at all. Some men claimed that saying things made them true. Well, many men who said they were rich still died poor. Nox said he was cool, but that sun showed him he was a liar.

He fell, toppling forward into the sand. He hadn't

even fully realised he'd lost his balance until the ground told him. And the ground didn't whisper. He could barely even utter a groan. His tongue stuck to the inside of his mouth, desperate for moisture. Maybe that was dying first, so he couldn't say to himself that he was alive.

He saw shimmering blue on the horizon, but on the third blink it turned out to be the merging of the sky and the sand. He swamped down the last of his waterskins, which brought him back just enough to trek on for another half mile.

But the sun was overhead, barbecuing him good. He could feel it even through his hat, burrowing through the stitches. His head was foggy. He craved another drink. It didn't matter what kind. He looked for some fishhook barrel cacti, but all he could see were the poisonous type. Oh, they had liquid all right. White, noxious, stomach-churning liquid. That'd help the sun kill you faster.

And then, just after falling for the second time, he saw what he craved: a body of water far ahead, with lush trees and bushes growing around it, and what looked like animals sipping from the pond. He tested his eyes, blinking rapidly, then closing them for a long moment to see if it'd disappear when he glanced again. It didn't. It was everything he needed, and yet he didn't feel like he had the energy to get to it.

"You'll make it," he barked again, feeling the grit on his tongue. It wasn't quite a lie now, because the truth was just within reach. He just hoped he didn't die on the doorstep.

He pushed on.

The oasis taunted him on the horizon. You see, it was part of the land—and that meant it wasn't your friend. He couldn't don the feather of the tamba bird and do the dance of the Ootana. He had no right to connect to the land like they did, any more than the criminals had any right to walk away from him. He had his badge and the tribes had theirs. His let him wander the desert, but it didn't make the land a friend.

And yet there it was, a little closer, that great bucket of moisture waiting to be sipped. The thought of it made him a little delirious, as if he was addicted to that refreshing pool. But then everyone was. When you gave it up, you gave up the ghost as well.

He dragged himself across the desert, not quite inch by inch, but grain by grain. He left a trail of blood behind him, which he knew someone would soon follow. But that didn't matter while he bled out. It didn't matter while the sun toasted him dry. It didn't matter when there was nowhere to run, and barely anywhere to crawl. He left it all behind him, grain by grain, drip by drip. Precious blood. Precious sweat. Precious tears. Isn't it funny how they were all liquid?

But what was stranger was that, as he crawled towards it, the oasis almost seemed to crawl to him. As desperate as he was for it, that made him distrust his vision all the more. It was one thing to die in the desert. It was something else to die thinking you were gonna live.

But the Coilhunter's trained eyes didn't deceive him. That oasis *did* move, and the animals sipping from it didn't. That was no natural body of water. It was a Roaming Oasis, a crawling mechanical beast, on which sat a diorama of what every thirsty drifter ever wanted. It was a fake deer, a false bird—but the water was real. It was housed in a great big vat beneath the surface, behind where the industrious trader sat, palm waiting.

Nox sat up and did some waiting of his own. There was no point wasting energy crawling when the water was crawling to him. You were half-lucky if you found one of these, because you wouldn't find much else out in the wilds. But the other half was the price. It sure as hell wouldn't be cheap. Why, it was daylight robbery, as if the day wasn't already cruel enough. The night wasn't a whole lot better. If you could, you'd live in the twilight between them, straddling the place between life and death.

The Roaming Oasis cranked and crawled. It was like a crab, except it moved forward too. You could barely see its stumpy limbs, which sank into the sand. The tops of them were dusted over, to help the illusion. You see, those traders wanted you to think it was the real thing. If you knew it was them, you'd know you were going to get robbed.

The machine halted a yard away from Nox. A shutter opened, revealing a short, stout fellow with a thick moustache and even thicker eyebrows. Nox guessed he didn't need shades.

"Well, howdy, there," the man said. "The name's Warren, but Wet Warren they call me, on account o' the business." He knocked his knuckles off the edge of the window.

"Well, I'm guessin' you know who I am," Nox said,

forcing himself up. He tried to seem intimidating, but that was hard when his legs almost buckled. He noticed two turrets on the front of the vessel, which looked like they'd buckle him quicker.

"Oh, you could be anyone," Wet Warren said with a knowing smile. "Alls I know is that you sir look mighty thirsty. Where you headin', son?"

"To the Crescent," Nox replied. "And yeah," he added, smacking his lips. "I could drink a lake. Ya got one?"

"Canyon Crescent? Why, that ain't far off where I'm headin'. What are the chances?"

What were the chances indeed? By now, Nox had enough wounds to make him paranoid. If someone was going his way, he couldn't help but wonder if they were going there because they were following his trail. But paranoia had a way of destroying a mind, and Nox knew he needed whatever allies he could find. He needed to find them while he still had some mind left.

"Now, about that drink," Warren said.

"How much?" Nox asked.

"Ten coils," Wet Warren said. "For a half-fill."

"That's too much."

"It is what it is." Warren grinned. "It's not like you have a choice."

Nox tapped his fingers on his right pistol. "I could just take it." It was easy to say that compared to doing it, not in his condition right now, and saying it was hard enough. His sandpaper throat wore his words down until they didn't quite sound so menacing.

But Warren didn't budge. Instead, the twin turrets on the front of the Oasis automatically turned in towards the Coilhunter.

"I could just take your life," Warren said. "And then your coils."

"Well then," Nox replied, taking his hand away slowly from his gun. "Isn't it good for the both of us that we're both honest men?"

Warren smiled, a real one this time. "Why, yessir, it is! So, how many fills?"

"Just the one," Nox said, handing over his canister. It was better than handing over his life.

"No more waterskins?"

"No more coils," Nox said, slinging the little pouch of iron onto the counter. He couldn't help but note the irony that he, the fabled Coilhunter, was out of coils, nor the fact that every passing day the reward on his head went up for someone else. He almost wondered if he could claim that prize himself.

"Well," Warren said, "at least you had these." He emptied the bag of coils, counting them quickly by scooping each down into a box behind the counter. Nox heard a lot of clinks down there. Wet Warren had made his fortune out here in the desert, buying expensive water from the Dew Distributors and selling it at ten times the price to the desperate.

Nox swamped down half the skin.

"Pace yourself," Warren said. "There's still miles to go."

Nox nodded to the man, then turned to leave.

"Well, you have a good day now," Warren said. "And try and not die of thirst."

The Oasis plodded off into the haze, looking

for some other sucker with too many coils and too much air in his waterskins. Wet Warren must've felt pretty smug inside, sipping at his leisure, letting his mechanical beast chug along. While he was counting his wealth, the vehicle moved a little slower. All those extra coils added to the weight.

But then so did the Coilhunter, perched on top like another animal. He lay down beneath the fake deer, which was just a wooden cut-out up close. It was good to get off the sand, to rest his weary limbs. It was good to get out of the eye of the sun, and the eyes of everyone else. As he took a sip of his own, creating a momentary oasis in his mouth, he was feeling a little smug as well.

Chapter Twenty-one

CANYON CRAWL

The Roaming Oasis coasted the Canyon Crescent for about three miles before it started to veer off in a direction the Coilhunter wasn't going. He slipped away silently, vanishing into the exhaust fumes. He wouldn't have minded if it'd brought him right to his doorstep, but this was good enough. It gave him the rest he needed. He had a gut feeling that it wouldn't last long, and that wasn't just the wound talking.

He slipped through a thin pass into the canyon, which was actually a series of canyons meeting together in a moon-shaped curve. The passages varied in size, some barely enough to squeeze through, others wide enough to fit a landship. It was a place to get lost in.

And it was where his hideout, his workshop, was.

He was glad of the shadow the great granite cliffs cast inside the passage. The sun was already starting to set, but that didn't stop it trying to throw a final lashing glimmer your way. This was a refuge for all sorts, for the wildlife and wild men. In bygone years it was home to a tribe. There were still faint markings high up on the cliff walls, where the tribespeople edged out on thin ledges. A pocket of holes here and there were the work of nature's slow erosion, but they became dwelling places. It was one of these, a cavern, that served as Nox's home. Of sorts. To him, it was just the place he waited between the moment he'd died inside and the moment his body would catch up.

He walked the initial trail for just shy of an hour before the first bullet fired.

He dived under a ledge, pressing his back against the cliff. It was hard to see so far up, but he knew the bullet came from the plateau above. They were shooting far, and their accuracy suffered, but Nox didn't exactly have a lot of places to dance through the bullets. They came in number, like rain. You couldn't afford to get wet.

Nox stayed in the shadows, beneath the outcroppings. The bullets edged closer, not by design, but by chance. Yet chance wasn't your ally either. One grazed by his face, leaving a little hole in his hat for the light to shine through. You'd think they wanted the sun to finish him off.

But who were *they*? It was clear that there was more than one of them. Three bullets clipped the ground in almost perfect unison, and few had guns that could fire simultaneous rounds. There was a posse up there with a good vantage and a better supply of ammunition. They didn't care that they were wasteful. After all, they'd be cashing in on a fat bounty soon.

Nox was still a ways off from his hideout, and he didn't like the idea of showing them the way. Some might've known he travelled those paths, and might've even suspected he made a dwelling there, but he didn't want to give them certainty—least of all when they were looking to gun him down.

He sidled along the passage, until there was no roof above him. Then he dashed out into the open, skipping through the bullets, with his guitar held above his head. Well, that only helped pinpoint him easier, and the lead rain became a downpour. When he ran, they ran along the clifftops with him, firing as they went, leaving little pockets in his footprints.

Nox reached a part of the canyon where a bridge of rock crossed between. He hid under there for a moment, planning his next step. Those cliffs were too high to scale, and the wind was against him.

So, he waited.

The shots slowed, then stopped. He could hear their voices far above, mixed with the gossip of the wind. It seemed like they were arguing, snarling like wolves. That's the thing about coyotes who'd found a corpse. They were willing to make each other new ones in the fight for it.

He heard the lash of a rope and the grunt of a man. Someone was lowering themselves down. That was a foolish thing to do, but greed eats away at your logic, until all you see is gold, iron, or coils. The world of Altadas had proved that those things were passing things. There were graveyards of gold to prove it.

The man swung under the bridge and Nox seized him with both arms before throwing him to the ground. He cast away the man's pistols. He didn't have a whole lot of strength left, but he had enough to jam his own pistol in the man's jaw.

"You curious?" he asked. "Why, my pistol's

curious what's in that skull o' yours. Now, let me guess. A *whole* lotta nothin'. Oh, but to find out for sure."

"I ... I ... no, please!"

"You what? No, what? Oh, I'm glad you at least have some manners." He forced the gun in deeper, deep enough to leave the print of the barrel. That man could wear that like a badge. When the others asked him what it was, and he lied, that same mark would form on his soul. He'd see it again in the afterlife.

"P-p-please don't shoot!" the man begged.

"You give me one good reason." That was all. Nox really wanted it, so he didn't have to kill another man just trying to make his fortune. See, they didn't know he wasn't bad. Some of them might've even thought they were doing God's work. Well, if they were, Nox'd have a message for God too.

"I have a wife," the man said.

"Go on."

"And a child. A girl."

"And?"

"And ... and ... and that's it."

"That's two. Give me a third."

"I ... uh ... eh—"

"Have ya got a conscience?"

The man nodded frantically.

"Well, then," Nox said, pulling him to his feet. "You go out there and tell your boys that I'm a good man who got a raw deal. Those posters are wrong. They're lies. Y'hear me? The letters are lies. You let my mercy be your proof. Will ya do that?"

"Y-y-yes."

"Oh, don't let your manners die now."

"Oh, y-yes, thank, uh, please … thank you."

"You go out there now and let them know," Nox insisted, and he did it with the gun.

"I will."

"You make 'em believe it."

"I will!"

"'Cause it's the truth. Y'hear?"

"I do. I will. I'll tell them."

Nox let the man go, and he scampered out from under the bridge, like a wild animal who'd just been freed from a snare. That was when one of his boys up top shot him, so eager for the Coilhunter's head. You see, the coyote spirit can be found in men.

Chapter Twenty-two

DOORSTEP DRIFTER

Nox used the man's death as a distraction, darting out of his hiding place. He raced through the next passage, which was wide and open. They followed alongside him, taking pot shots, until he turned sharply down a different canyon trail. They had to leap over the gap to follow him there.

But they followed.

He kept running, rolling under a ledge here and there, which helped when the gunfire came down heavy. Then he came to a long, wide passage where he could duck low under an outcropping on the attackers' side, hiding him from their shots. He could hear them muttering something above, and he suspected they were sending some around the far side for a better vantage.

In time, he reached his hidden workshop, dug deep into the canyon wall. He'd covered the huge metal door with a sheet of sand and shards of rock. The shadows did the rest. He waited until he couldn't hear the men above. He hoped they'd continued farther on.

He was about to open the door when he saw a boot sticking out from under an old blanket in a little cavern nearby. He sneaked up close to it and pointed his pistol at the straw hat covering the man's face. Someone'd camped out there for him, and he'd caught them before they caught him.

"Thought you'd catch me at home, huh?" Nox rasped.

The man stirred, and the hat fell down from his face.

Except it wasn't a man. It was Handcart Sally.

Chapter Twenty-three

WAR IN THE WORKSHOP

"Why, Sally, you're lucky I'm not a shoot-first kinda man with you there hidin' like that."

Sally shook off her sleep, rolling her shoulders. Her golden curls tumbled off them. "That ain't luck, Nox. I know what kinda man you are."

"What're you doin' here?"

"I was worried." She wiped a knuckle beneath her eye, almost like she was trying to remove the bit of the soot that always seemed to get on her face. She was a working girl, someone who wasn't afraid of the dirt. That was how she met the Coilhunter, when he was trying to clean it up.

"Well, you shouldn't be," Nox replied.

Sally scoffed. "You have half the Wild North after you."

"I can handle half."

"Maybe you can, but … I just had to check that you were okay."

"Well," he said, pausing. "I'm okay."

He grabbed the handle of the door into his workshop and heaved it open. It ground and creaked, making an almighty racket that would've surely brought those hunters back if they were in earshot.

Yet he'd barely pulled one door open when he heard Sally gasp, and saw a pistol coming out of the dark inside, pointing right at his head.

He grabbed the attacker's arm, twisting the man around so that the bullet struck the granite wall outside. He knocked the gun to the floor. Sally reached for her rifle, but there was no shooting the attacker while he was rolling about with the Coilhunter inside.

Nox pushed the man back into a table of tools, casting everything to the floor. They danced over them, slipping and tripping, shoving violently back and forth. Black smoke erupted from his mask, trailing about in spirals as they turned in place.

The man reached for one of Nox's pistols, but Nox grabbed his wrist and clenched it tight, keeping that gun holstered. He smacked the man in the jaw, which got him an answering punch that the attacker quickly regretted. The Coilhunter's jaw was a metal mask, and you could punch that all you liked.

They pushed each other through the connecting caverns, into the darkness of Nox's domain. The attacker got Nox on his back, only for Nox to throw him over his head. The man didn't tumble, but he rolled with a clang into the foot of a parked monowheel. It groaned in response.

The man got up and wiped his bloodied mouth. There was a grim look in his eyes, replacing the greed. He charged at Nox, pushing him back into a row of shelves, where Nox kept a display of old toys he'd made. The shelves toppled, and those toys fell down, smashing on the ground.

Nox saw them and growled. He almost reached

for his pistols, but instead he grabbed the man's head and bashed his mask against it. The man stumbled to his knees, only to receive a kneecap in the nose. He fell onto his back, and Nox leapt upon him, driving his fists into his face with a fury you hoped to never see. Nox roared as he punched, until the man's eyes barely blinked, until his face was matted with blood, and his hands no longer tried to fight back.

And Nox kept going.

"He's gone," Sally said, edging in, placing a hand on Nox's shoulder.

He shrugged it off, taking another punch.

"Nox!"

Nox paused, his fist held high. He looked at it, with his now-red glove. He looked back at the face of his attacker, that face that'd summoned hate in him. He looked at the broken pieces of the toys nearby, and his lip trembled. He was glad Sally couldn't see it behind the mask.

"He's gone, Nox," she whispered. "It's okay. He's gone."

Nox pushed himself away from the body, resting his back at a nearby wall. He held his hands out before him. "No," he said, his voice wavering. "It's … it's not okay."

"He got what he deserves," Sally said. "I was preppin' to shoot him myself."

"This isn't me," Nox said.

"Well, who is it then?"

Nox took off his gloves and cast them aside. He gathered some of the toy parts to him and held them close. There were the broken sails of a little metal windmill, the crushed carriage of a toy train, a wooden bear carrying cymbals, with one of his ears lost in the pool of blood nearby.

Nox's eyes welled up.

Sally crouched down beside him, placing her rifle on the ground.

"It doesn't get any easier, does it?" she said.

The Coilhunter shook his head.

"Y'know, the past doesn't change," Sally said. "It's the future that does that."

"Well, what future is there now? I'm supposed to be better than them."

"You are! None of this changes that."

Nox let out a long sigh, dropping the toy pieces onto his lap. He looked around the cavern, with its faint electric light, with the monowheel ready, with the body on the floor.

"I'm fightin' to prove I'm a good man, and here's a man dead in my home."

"He attacked you," Sally said. "Do you think he would've given you mercy? Do you think he would've given me some? If this were reversed, and it was our bodies there on the floor, do you think he'd be sittin' here with a worried conscience? No, he'd be takin' everything he could and troddin' over it all. Some men deserve to die, Nox. You know that. He well and proved he was bad when he came in here. Do I have to get Luke to draw you a poster before you believe it?"

Nox sighed. "No." He shook his head. "It's just … I didn't like that feelin' there, that rage. It didn't feel like justice then. It felt like something else."

"Well, the fact that you can tell the difference makes you better than them."

Nox turned to her, his eyes grim. "A few more days of bein' hunted and I might not be."

Chapter Twenty-four

CHECKIN' IN

The Coilhunter searched his place, finding a hole in the door leading up a shaft to the plateau above, where he kept his windmill, generator, and antennae, some of the machinery that kept the business of the law running. The door had been blasted open, and there were likely more hunters parked outside. Nox boarded it up quick, hoping for a moment's rest. You'd think you could count on that in your own home, but everyone was a kind of drifter, temporarily nailed down. The shifting sands, and man's shifting nature, didn't make it last for long.

When he was certain his workshop was empty, except for his tools, toys, and weapons, and him and Handcart Sally, he sat down with her at a table with less clutter on it than most. He scooped aside some tools and rolled up his schematics. There was only one person out there better than him at making vehicles, and that man was dead. The desert didn't want new things.

"You want a drink?" Nox asked.

"D'ya even have to ask?"

Nox poured two whiskeys. He was hesitant when unlatching his mask, revealing the scars. It wasn't embarrassment, as some thought. It was shame. He would've worn them proudly if he'd gotten his kids out, if he'd gotten his wife out, if he'd even saved one of them. But he failed, and Emma had paid. Little Ambrose had paid. Little Aaron had paid. He'd arrived too late, having spent a long night in his workshop at Loggersridge. Now he spent all his nights here in this new workshop, or out chasing folk who started fires.

Sally swamped down her glass. "I needed that."

Nox did the same. He felt he needed the bottle.

He topped up both glasses. He knew soon he'd be topping up his ammunition and returning to the battleground. You savoured the little moments in-between, because they were all you got. Life'd tried to take them too.

He suddenly thought about Luke and Laura. "Where are the kids?"

"They're with my sister."

"At that whorehouse?"

"They'll be safe there, Nox. Safer than you."

"God, Sally."

"Hey, don't you judge me. I've been through my own hell too, y'know. It hasn't been easy for them either. We're fendin' off raiders on the ranch, left, right and centre. Luke said it reminded him of home. I don't think he meant it in a good way."

"I could have—"

"No, Nox. We're doin' fine." She paused. "Not everyone needs a saviour."

He sighed. "Except maybe me."

"Well, it's lucky I'm here then, huh?" She smiled.

"You should stay outta this. It's too dangerous."

"Well, I'm in it now."

"No, you're not. You should ride back to the ranch."

"Maybe I should, but I won't. Not yet."

Nox grumbled. It there was anyone more stubborn than he was, it was Sally.

"How'd you get down here? Did you take your horse? He won't be safe in the canyon."

"I tied him at the step of the northern pass. He wouldn't come into the canyon. Big old scaredy-cat, that horse."

"That's Ootana horses for you. They spook easily."

"You got that right." Sally looked around the room. "Why don't you call Porridge? He could give you shelter in the sky for a bit."

"He's out of signal. Last I heard, he was doin' deals with the Resistance at sea. But even if he wasn't, this is my burden."

"It's mine now too."

"Well, it shouldn't be. Don't you see? A man like me is meant to be alone. Besides, Sally, those kids need you now. What if you die out here, helpin' me?"

"You could stay at the ranch," Sally suggested, "until all this blows over."

"But it won't blow over. It'll just bring it all to your ranch. I can't do that, and you can't do that either. It isn't about us anymore, Sally."

Sally sighed, nodding solemnly.

Nox paused. "How are they, anyway?"

"Hmm?"

"The kids. Luke and Laura. How're they?"

"They're good, for the most part. It took them

some time to settle in."

"About as long as it took you to settle down?" Nox asked.

Sally laughed. "Not that long. Hell, I'm not entirely sure I've settled."

"You're doin' fine. Better than most."

"Only 'cause I fight for it, Nox. I had one genuine girl come up to buy a horse. Called me 'ma'am' an' everythin'. The rest wanted to take 'em, and I sent 'em packin'. Did you know Luke's a crack shot?"

"Is he, now?" Nox said, smiling. "Wouldn't touch a gun with me."

"Maybe he misses you."

"Well, he's gonna have to keep on missin'. You know I can't have that life."

"Why, Nox? Why won't you let yourself love again? Why won't you let yourself *live* again? Don't pretend there's nothin' between us. It ain't all just desert."

He stared into her eyes, and, for once, his own were not grim. "I'm not pretendin', Sally. Yeah, maybe I feel somethin'. Underneath all this, I'm still just a man. But I can't go through that all again. I can't put you through it either. I can't put the kids through it too. You see what I attract. Trouble's my shadow. You step too close to me and it'll be yours as well."

"You're one broken man," Sally said, sighing. Maybe she thought she could patch him up, one little kiss at a time.

Nox held up one of his toys, damaged beyond repair. "This whole damn world is broken. I'm tryin' to fix it."

Sally turned to him. "Why don't you try to fix yourself?"

Nox cast the toy aside. "Some things just can't be salvaged."

They both sighed in unison.

"So, your sister," Nox said. "She still turnin' tricks?"

"She has a good life, Nox. You know what Ruby's like. She's good to the girls."

"I know what she's like all right. That's why I'd worry about Laura. Hell, *and* Luke."

"She made a promise."

"Well, she sure better keep it, Sally, or I might have to get Luke's sketch of her and put it up to replace my own."

"Speakin' of which," Sally said, "how do you plan to get all yours taken down? Who's the one who put your head up there in the first place?"

"I don't know, but I've got a few leads. I was kinda hopin' I could interrogate this guy too."

"There'll be more of 'em," Sally assured him.

"Oh, I know that. His posse is still outside on the plateau."

"What're you gonna do 'bout 'em?"

"Somethin' different than this one, I hope. Speakin' o' which, I suppose I better bury him."

"Wish I had my handcart," Sally said, but she forced her smile back into a frown when Nox shook his head.

So, Nox dragged that body outside and glanced up to see if anyone was waiting. It didn't seem they were. Maybe they'd gotten the message, intended or not, that Nox was going to fight. He dug a hole a few yards down in the softer earth, where the soil was sheltered from the sun.

Sometimes when you buried a man, you buried a bit of your conscience as well. You had to, in order to survive. What made you different in the Wild North wasn't that you had a conscience, but just how much of it you had left.

Chapter Twenty-five

RIDIN' THE CRESCENT

Nox slept for a few hours, and had his usual restless dreams. The fire was there. The screams were there. The only thing that was different was the odd feeling that at some point in the night, someone else was there, stroking his face.

He got up in the early morning, while it was still dark, and got to work on his supplies. He loaded up his spare monowheel, but he wasn't content with that. He attached twin grapnel launchers to the sides of it, having learnt just how handy they were in a pinch. He also replaced the ones on his arms, and reloaded his belt. He kept Shotgun Samson's shells for good measure. He brought the kind of toys he intended to break.

"I'll drop you off somewhere," Nox said, climbing into the monowheel.

"Yeah," she replied. He could see she was fighting the urge to add: *You can drop me off where you're goin'.* If it'd been a year ago, when her circumstances were different, she would've fought side by side with him. But she'd settled, and it didn't ever look like he would.

She climbed on behind him, wrapping her arms around his waist. He flinched, and the worry in her eyes returned. She knew well that beneath his shirt and coat, there were many wounds. You couldn't count the ones to his heart.

He edged out the door, shoving it closed behind him. The locks clicked tight.

"What if they come back?" Sally asked.

"I've made *adjustments* for that." He cranked a lever on the monowheel, which opened two wide panels on the top.

"A shield," she said. "Nice."

"It'll be nicer if we don't need it."

He revved the engine. The exhaust poured out its black fog, adding to the darkness of the night. It wouldn't be long now till dawn, and maybe the roar of the engine was what would wake the sun.

The monowheel rolled off, picking up speed quick. Nox turned on the headlights, which showed the edge of rocks. He only needed a little light. He knew that journey well, and knew it better on his trusty steed.

But light does bad things too, like attract moths and men. They barely got a few yards before the gunfire started. If the hunters slept, well, they slept on their triggers.

Nox was glad of his new shield, which blocked several shots. Others, he evaded, swinging this way and that, turning sharply around bends in the canyon path. The men followed, or at least their guns did, and they kept on shooting as if their bullets were sand. In the Wild North, they were just as plentiful.

Then Nox came to a thinner passage, which would've ripped off the monowheel's shields. He cranked them down just in time as the vehicle darted into the crevice. He even had to pull his legs in tight to stop the wall tearing through his jeans.

The hunters followed, making the most of it. They aimed their rifles down straight, and some of them even straddled the cliffs, with one foot on either side.

That was when Handcart Sally pointed her own rifle up.

She fired, and Nox started in his seat.

"What the hell are ya doin'?" he croaked.

"Have a guess!"

He reached back, yanking the rifle from her. "We're not doin' it that way."

"Well, they ain't playin' your game, Nox. You should play by *their* rules."

But Nox'd already done enough of that. Now he wanted to play by his own. He took a grapnel launcher form his belt, one of the new designs. It hadn't been tested, and it was a deal heavier than his usual kind. But now was as good a time as any to put it to the test.

He glanced up, catching sight of a silhouette dashing back and forth across the cliffs, with the first glimmers of morning catching its steel soles. Nox pointed the grapnel up and fired it just ahead of where the man was running. It flew up, the wire unravelling, and a bar extended from the hook at the top, catching either side of the canyon. The hunter ran right into it, as if he'd set upon his own trap, and he went tumbling down the ravine, with the wire caught around his leg. He yelled. Then he dangled, and his rifle clattered down behind the monowheel below.

Sally scoffed. "Would've been quicker to shoot

'im."

"I did."

Nox drove on, twisting and turning. The mono-wheel leant with him, and Sally hung on all the tighter. The shots subsided as they came to a wider passage, and Nox was able to put the shield panels back up, blocking the bullets of the sun. They came up to the mouth of the canyon, leading back out into the vast expanse.

That was when a bomb dropped right in front of them.

Chapter Twenty-six

LAST MAN STANDING

There was nowhere to turn to avoid the blast. Even if Nox jammed on the breaks, the monowheel would've struck the explosives. He could accelerate and get it over with, or he could find another way out. The only other way was up.

So he didn't stop, and he didn't push forward any faster. Instead, he pulled two levers into place, which unlocked his seat.

"Hang on," Nox said.

The seat swung back, until it, and the engine, and pretty much everything else, pointed upwards. That included the twin grapnel launchers he'd just installed. The wheel continued, and the fuse of the bomb burned low. Just seconds before the boom, Nox fired the hooks straight up, right into the cliff face, and the wires hauled the vehicle up and through the gush from the explosion.

The blast pushed the vehicle up, even as the wires pulled, sending it straight up past the level of the cliffs. It was then that Nox leant the vehicle to the side and landed it on the plateau where the bomber stood. He snapped the wires, yanked the levers again, and his seat slid back into place.

The bomber looked at him in shock, clutching another unlit stick of dynamite.

Nox revved and launched forward. He grabbed the coiled rope from the side of the monowheel and swung it hard, lassoing that bomber's neck and yanking him to the ground. He dropped his dynamite into the crevice, and he yelped as he was dragged along behind the monowheel. Nox didn't want to kill these men, but that didn't mean he wouldn't hurt them.

He kept going, skirting the edge of the plateau, enough for the scree to tumble. He took a four-barrel shotgun from a slot on the monowheel and pointed it at the next hunter, who was raising his rifle. All four barrels had different shells from Samson's supply, and Nox'd made the gun so he could select the chamber. He fired, blasting the rifle out of the man's hands, and leaving him with a handful of rock salt to remember him by. Nox had his own memories to know damn well that it hurt.

He evaded the shots of the next two hunters, who were about ten yards apart, one on the edge, another farther in. Sally blasted the rifle from the hands of one, and Nox swerved the monowheel at the other, kicking up the dust in his face. He toppled backwards over the cliff, screaming, until Nox fired one of his arm-mounted grappling hooks around the man's waist—then he screamed some more as the recoil pulled him back up to the Coilhunter.

Nox rolled to a halt and got out, unravelling the hook and wire, letting it lock back into place. He hauled that man up by his collar and hung him over the edge until his feet dangled.

"Tell me why I shouldn't drop you," he barked.

All the man could do was mumble and yell, crying out for help. There wasn't anyone there to help him.

Nox cast him back onto the plateau. He took the fallen rifle and emptied the chamber into the chasm, before tossing the gun down after. Then he moved to the next one, the man he'd been hauling along by the throat. He took his knife out, and that man yelped like a dog. He cut the rope and let him free, taking his pistol and putting it into the back of his belt.

"You go now," he said, "and you better hope I don't ever see your faces on posters. If you see mine, you pull those down quick, and you tell 'em I was merciful. You got me on a good day, boys, because that mercy wears out quick."

He got back on and revved the engine, sending out thick black smoke right into those scoundrel's faces. They hacked up their lungs, but they were lucky they were still breathing at all.

Nox drove on, until he came to a canyon trail that turned back and forth down to the sand below. He had to be careful going down there, with its thin paths and steep falls.

But more than anything, he had to be careful of the silhouette of a man on horseback far below, riding slow and steady upwards, blocking the way.

"Looks like we have more company," Sally said.

"Yeah," Nox replied, reaching for his belt.

Chapter Twenty-seven

CHANCE OAKLEY

Nox waited for that man to journey up, but he didn't journey quick. It was a treacherous path for horses, and those that weren't born brave had a hard time being bred it. Yet that man knew his horses, and he seemed to calm and comfort his mount as they went. It was a blonde sorrel, with a majestic brown mane, like something a tribal chief might ride—like something even Nox might ride, if he weren't too attached to the monowheel.

Nox didn't let him come up fully. If you had the high ground like this, you didn't sacrifice it easily. It'd be a foolish man who drew on him from that path, but the Wild North was full of the graves of foolish men.

The man halted two turns of the path down from where Nox sat with one buckled boot planted firmly on the ground. On the other side, the side the rider couldn't see, Nox had unbuckled his holster. His fingers itched.

The man looked up, holding his hat on to save it from the wind. He squinted at the morning sunlight. He was white-haired, with a thick white moustache that fell down both sides like a waterfall. The rest of his face was crags and crevices. Why, you might as well've said he'd mapped the desert there.

But it was his eyes that told the most. This man had seen things. He had a wizened look, which was far apart from the crazed look the other hunters had. He wasn't here for a bounty. Nox wasn't quite sure if that was worse.

He tipped his hat to Nox. "G'day, drifter." He took it off for Sally. "Ma'am."

Nox didn't respond. He kept his hand at his hip, ready. He noted that this stranger hadn't got pistols on his belt, just a big old rifle strapped to his back. It'd take longer to draw that than to drop to the ground from the Coilhunter's gun. And the drop was big. That poor old horse must've had a premonition. It looked nervously at Nox, like an onlooker watching two men face off in the streets.

"You look like you've had it rough," the stranger observed. He had to shout the words up. "Not you, mind," he added, nodding to Sally. She eyed him coldly.

"If you're gonna draw," Nox said, "then draw."

"I'd never draw on a man I didn't know."

Nox would. You see, you mightn't know the person, but you could take a pretty good guess about their motives. Rarely were they anything good.

"But then," the stranger said, with a twinkle in his eye, "I do know you, don't I? Nathaniel Osley Xander, in the flesh."

"More or less," Nox replied, though he felt a lot less in the flesh now than he did before this hunt began. He didn't ask how the man knew him. Nox's name was like sand. It got everywhere. That was partly why that poster with his face was doing so much damage. Everyone knew him.

"Though I don't quite know you, ma'am," the rider said to Sally.

"Let's keep it that way," she replied.

"And what do I call you?" Nox shouted down.

"Oh, Thomas Oakley, if you will, or just my family name, if you like. Don't quite got all your titles, now, but some call me Chance Oakley."

"And why's that?" Nox asked. Not a single word of this made his trigger finger itch any less.

"'Cause I give people one more chance than maybe they deserve. But then, who am I to judge? So, I try not to. I just try to do a little good. Lord, ain't nothin' we can do but try."

Nox didn't quite agree with that. When he went hunting for criminals, he didn't try. He got them, and he got them good. Of course, running the other way wasn't quite so easy. There, he was trying, and trying hard.

"I'm a drifter," Oakley said, "just like you. Ain't got quite the recognition you have, mind, but you could say I'm a little famous. Just a little, mind."

"Well, how come I never heard of you?"

Oakley smiled. "'Cause I ain't *infamous*."

Nox didn't smile back, not with his mouth and not with his eyes. Some had tried to talk their way into him lowering his guard, and he'd made those mistakes before, but he didn't try to learn from them. He learned them quick.

"Here," Oakley said, reaching inside his pocket.

"For that dry mouth o' yours."

He threw something up. It was small, like a stone—or a bomb. Nox instinctively drew his gun and shot it to pieces. Those pieces rained down on Chance Oakley.

"Hell, now," the rider said, shielding his face with his hat.

"You said you knew me," Nox replied. "Then you should've known not to do that."

"It's just boiled candy, Nathaniel." Oakley took another out of his pocket, holding it up to the sunlight, before popping it into his mouth. "Helps keep the juices flowin'. Don't tell me you don't need that out here."

"I'll have one," Sally yelled down. She caught the next one Oakley threw, and Nox had to fight the urge to blast that one apart as well. He rolled his eyes at Sally.

"What?" she said, before popping the candy in her mouth.

"If you want another one yourself, Nathaniel, I'll throw it up," Oakley said, "but I don't expect you to use it as target practice."

"I'm good, thanks," Nox croaked. The grit in his voice betrayed just how much he could've done with a mouth-watering sweet.

"Well, I know you're *good*," Oakley said. "Everyone knows that."

"Doesn't feel like it these last few days." Nox paused. "Why're you out here?"

"Same as you," Oakley said. "Driftin'. Well, not quite the same, I'd wager."

"I ain't a bettin' man."

"But are you a runnin' man?"

"So, you know."

"Hard not to know, Nathaniel. They've got posters everywhere."

"I didn't do it."

"I know," Oakley said. "Or, at least, I'm willin' to give you a chance. You see, I heard gunfire up here, and I knew this was Coilhunter territory, and, moreover, I knew that the Coilhunter might've gotten himself into a spot of bother. So, here I came, ridin' on up."

"Not many men out there who'd ride into another man's fight," Nox said.

"No siree, there ain't. But that's what you've been doin' all these years, right?"

"Forgive me if I seem blunt," Nox said, "but I've had a few too many hunters on my trail to not be a mite suspicious of anyone else who wanders along."

"Well, that's mighty wise o' you, all things considered. I'd be in a similar boat myself, if we had seas out here to sail in."

"Let me test 'im," Sally said quietly to Nox.

"If you think you can."

"I know I can."

Sally hopped off the monowheel and climbed down a bit. As she did, Chance climbed off his own steed and walked him up to meet her. He took off his hat to her again.

"Well, you've got manners," Nox shouted down. "At least I won't have to teach you 'em."

Oakley smiled. "'Bout alls I got is manners, but

those don't come cheap in these parts."

"No, they don't."

Sally largely ignored Oakley, focusing her attention on his horse instead. She rubbed its mane, and that old stallion whinnied joyfully.

"You look after him," she said.

"Oh, I try," Oakley said, "which is more than can be said o' most. You've got a regular old tribesman here without a tribe. That is, a tribesman in spirit, if you couldn't tell." He brushed the hair away from his pale face. Where it wasn't pale, it was red from the sun.

Sally led the horse up the remaining slope, right up next to Nox. He followed dutifully, as if his duty was a pleasure. Horses only did that when they liked their station, and who they'd been saddled with. And Sally knew her horses.

"He's good," she told Nox, not quite out of earshot of Oakley.

"Kind o' you to say so, ma'am," the drifter said.

Nox still didn't quite trust that man, but he trusted Sally. She'd earned his trust, and she hadn't broken it since. That was a rare thing, as rare as a man who keeps his word. And if you trusted someone, that was your word that you'd take their opinions to heart. So Nox did.

The horse nudged Nox on the shoulder gently.

"He likes you," Oakley said.

"Well, that's a first."

"Don't rightly know what he was called before, but I've been riding a month with him now and he hasn't let me down. So I've called him Old Reliable.

Huh, y'know, men should have names like that, that tell you who they are."

"They do," Nox said, "though mostly the bad ones."

Oakley offered to trot alongside Nox for a bit, give him a bit of company, and maybe make any would-be hunters think twice about coming their way. By rights, Nox alone should've scared them, but it's strange what a poster and a notion can do, especially when that notion combines the feeling of doing good with that one better feeling of being rich.

Nox dropped Sally off where she'd tied her horse, Old-timer Bill. It was funny how often folk named their horses Old. It was an odd kind of endearing. More than anything, though, it showed how you rarely said that of men. That was because most men died young.

"You be good now," he said.

"You be safe now," she replied.

There was a moment where it seemed like they might hug, but the moment passed. It passed liked everything between them passed, in the silence, in the no man's land between their bodies. Nox needed that buffer zone, because that was where he kept the dead.

Sally got on her horse and rode away. She looked back once, but she continued on. Nox knew it was for the best, but that didn't mean it didn't sting. He knew it stung her too, maybe even more than him. But that was the way of things, like the unwritten codes of a gunslinger. A lone wolf endangers the pack.

Chapter Twenty-eight

SECOND CHANCES

They say first impressions tell you who folk really are. Well, that wasn't always true. If your first impression of Nox was his face on a Wanted poster, you'd think he was a criminal. It was just as well there were some—a mere handful, it seemed—who were willing to give a second glance.

"What were you, before you became a drifter?" Nox asked.

Oakley smirked. "Can't you guess?"

"Well, I'd guess prospector, but I ain't a guessin' man."

"Well, you should be, because your guess is right on target there."

"Iron?"

"Gold. Back when it was worth somethin'."

"Back then, huh?"

"You know, I made myself a claim out here, and I set up shop with two of my good friends. We sunk our entire fortune into it, sold our old homes and all. Moved the families out. Made a little town around our site. We wanted for nothin' then, except maybe a bit o' peace and quiet, 'cause the news of gold brought bandits our way. But those were the good days, strange enough."

"Then the Regime came," Nox said.

Oakley sighed. "Then they came, and they built their Iron Empire overnight. You know, I was foolish enough to think the Resistance would hold them off, send 'em back to where they came from. I thought my gold'd keep its value. Shucks, you'd think you had a safe bet with what the Treasury hoarded. But even here, in this untouched part of Altadas, things changed quick. As soon as that Iron Emperor sat down on his throne, well, people got jittery. Coils were the new currency then, and that meant iron. So my little gold mine fell to ruin, and my town with it."

Nox shook his head. "That ain't right."

"No, it ain't, but that's history now. My wife upped and left. We never did have any little ones, so it made it easier, I guess. My two good friends left too, and took their families with them. I never did realise they only stayed for the gold. I thought … you know, I thought *I* was the gold."

"That's folks for ya."

"That's folks indeed," Oakley said. "And that's when I became a drifter. I'd settled down, and it'd unsettled itself from right under me. I went searchin' for who I am, and I met some tribes, and I went on some journeys—in the mind, even, though some say the soul. Taught me a few things 'bout life, so it did. I could've given up hope on folk, but I didn't. I knew not all out there were lookin' just for gold or iron. Some are lookin' for meanin'. And, you know, maybe I can help a little along the way."

"Well, that's mighty noble of you," Nox said.

"Maybe it is, but it ain't nothin' compared to the work you do."

They journeyed on for a bit, then set up camp and cooked beans over a small fire. The poor man's meat. Drifter food. Some said beans'd get you across the desert and back. Dead men said a lot of things.

"You're somethin' rare," Nox said. "Ain't many willin' to share their meals out here."

"Ain't many, no, but you go share a meal with someone, and chances are they'll go on and share theirs with someone else. Plays out like dominoes, Nathaniel. Good or bad. So we gotta make sure the first one's good."

"Some'd say that's dreamer talk."

"Well, it is," Oakley said, "but we all can dream, right?"

Nox didn't have those kind of dreams. He just had the nightmares.

Oakley wolfed down another bowl of beans. "I like to give folks a little nudge in the right direction."

"How's that workin' out?"

"Works well enough. Y'see, most haven't ever had a real good day. And if you keep wakin' up on the bad side of the bed, only to see the world is bad around you, well, it ain't any wonder that you're gonna be bad."

"That's why we gotta clean up the world."

"True enough, but there ain't just one way o' doin' it."

"I know a way that works."

"Well, so do I," Oakley said. "Folks deserve a chance. And I'm not just talkin' about second chances.

In these parts, we ain't even givin' 'em the first."

"And what if you give 'em that chance and they go on doin' bad anyway?"

Oakley smiled. "Well, that's where you come in."

Chapter Twenty-nine

A CHANCE TO DIE

They shared banter, and Nox felt some more relief from the hunt. But it didn't take long before Nox was faced with those same types he'd talked about. Their camp was soon assailed by a posse of mean-looking men, the kind whose faces told you they'd seen far too many knuckles. The kind of men who lived to start a fight.

"Hmm," Oakley grumbled, dousing the fire. He probably wished he'd done it sooner. It was the first time Nox felt like these new gun-toting folk weren't here for him.

"Trouble?" Nox asked.

"Always is."

"Oakley," the leader of the posse said. He was a tall man, towering over the others. He had a voice that towered too. "It's time you pay."

"What'd you do?" Nox asked.

"He stole my horse is what he did."

"I set him free," Oakley replied. "You were mistreatin' 'im, Ben."

That was Ben Budson, a rancher up in Oldtown, a small stone settlement from bygone years. He'd made himself into the town's mayor, and he did it by shouting loudest—and shooting first.

"Ain't none o' your business how I was treatin' my own property, Oakley," he said. "You went and stole, and there's a price to pay for that. It's a mighty higher price than you'd have paid if you just bought the horse fair and square."

And, by rights, that was true. There had to be some kind of law, even out here on the frontiers. If you did bad, then you should expect bad would be done to you. But Nox didn't like the look of these folk, and he was starting to think that maybe Oakley should be given a second chance.

Besides, *he* was the law.

"Let him buy it now, then," Nox said. If he'd had any coils left, he would've thrown them over. It was better than throwing bullets.

"It's too late for—wait. Ain't you the Coilhunter?"

They looked at him now with greedy eyes. That name rolled around their minds like it was a gambling table, and, like too many men who hunted the Coilhunter, they felt they'd gotten lucky. Maybe they thought they could tell the stories later of how they took down the Man with a Thousand Names.

Nox didn't confirm their suspicion. He didn't have to. His mask all but did it. If it didn't, his stance would've given it away. He always stood like he was ready for battle. And he was.

"You oughta go on back to where you came from," Nox said. "Back to where it's *safe*."

Ben looked at his compatriots, just a quick glance to and fro, but it was enough for Nox to see that they'd made their bets. They were putting it all on red.

Ben drew, but Nox drew first, blasting that gun right out of his hand. He fanned the hammer, spreading out the bullets between the four other men reaching for their pistols. It was just a warning shot to each, grazing their knuckles, lashing their guns back into their holsters.

They backed away.

"Now, that ain't right, there!" Ben bellowed.

"What you just did ain't right either."

"He can't just get away with stealin' horses like that."

"And he won't. Consider it my debt to pay, Ben. You give me a week and I'll get you twice that horse's worth."

"You won't survive the week, Coilhunter," Ben said. "And besides, that horse there is worth a lot."

That was a lie, sure as day, but Ben was a liar, and that was surer still. Nox would give twice what Oakley estimated, and that'd be it. If Ben were wise, which he clearly wasn't, he'd be happy with that. If he were wise, he wouldn't have said what he said next.

"We'll be back for you."

"Well, then," Nox said. "You better bring more guns."

Ben's posse turned and left, looking over their shoulders nervously. Nox stared them down until they were out of range.

"Thanks for that," Oakley said.

"Well, they asked for it."

"They did indeed, but thanks all the same."

"Do you make a habit outta stealin' horses?"

"Not a habit, no. Just call me a sucker for the eyes

of a mistreated fellow like this one."

"Better than callin' you a thief."

"Well, that depends on how you look at things," Oakley said, fanning himself with his hat. "I doubt Old Reliable sees it that way, at least. Either way, though, I owe you one. If I had much in the way of money, I'd pay you now. I'd rather pay you than them."

"Well, it's them you owe, not me."

"Still though," Oakley said. "If there's anythin' I can do, I'll do it."

Nox paused. "I'm lookin' for a man who wears a bowler hat. Ain't many of those nowadays."

"Well, then I'd start with old Bowler Bronson if I were you."

"Who's that?"

"Oh, he'll be a chief of the mines."

"Which mines?" Nox asked.

"Black Hand Quarry."

"Do you know the way?"

"Like I know my horses. If you need a partner, I have the time. Ain't got a lot else but time, and that's more than most. So, I'll saddle up with you, if you don't mind workin' with a thief, that is."

If you were picky about who you worked with in the Wild North, you'd be quickly left with no one to choose. You could try to pick the best of them, but you'd have to dig them up first.

Nox nodded to Oakley. "Well, then," he said. "Let's find out who's been drawin' pictures of me, and maybe I'll draw some o' my own."

Chapter Thirty

BLACK HAND QUARRY

They rode on to perhaps the largest iron mine in the whole of the Wild North: Black Hand Quarry. It was a sprawling complex, with nine-tenths of it deep underground. Slaves toiled there, sent by the Night Slavers, and when they dropped dead, they were left where they lay. In time, they became part of the mine as well.

It was run by the Black Hand Gang, who got their name from all the iron mines they operated across the Wild North, many of them servicing the Regime. They made currency, legally, when the Iron Empire was watching, and illegally when they weren't. Bowler Bronson, the best counterfeiter in all of Altadas, or so he claimed, was in charge. At least, he was the newest chief to dirty his hands. Gang warfare often meant you didn't stay long at the top. Nox meant to make that record even briefer.

Nox and Oakley stared down at the network of mine carts vanishing into the mine and reappearing out the farthest side, loaded to the brim with iron ore. The sun made the silhouettes of slaves blend in with the iron they were working on, as if they were just human ore waiting to be smelted. There were rumours of factories in Regime territory that did just that, but you never could be certain about the tales people told.

"It'll be hard to get in there," Oakley said, nodding to the sentries posted throughout. Some of them were perched on huge gun platforms, ready to take on anyone who tried to storm the mine. They were designed to gun down armies, not just two men.

"We'll need to sneak through."

They climbed down slowly, hiding behind the outcropping rocks. They scurried along, peeping out every now and then. Periodically, two guards would stroll by, and Nox and Oakley would freeze. When the guards turned their backs, the duo dashed from cover to cover. They studied the movements of the guards, the routes of the patrols, and the angles of the sentry guns. Nox mapped out his own way through, and Oakley left him to it.

In time, they reached one of the empty carts destined for the mine. Nox hopped inside, pulling the cloth cover over him. Oakley was just about to climb in too, when a guard called over.

"You there," he said. "Help us with this."

"I, uh—"

"We need help unloadin' here," the guard shouted over.

"Just one minute." Oakley leant over the cart, pretending he was fixing the cover. "They think I'm one o' them."

"Good," Nox whispered back. "You keep an eye out for Bronson. See if he comes out the other side."

Oakley pushed the cart down the track a bit,

stopping when a group of slaves ran over to help. Then that drifter went to help unload the ore, casting around old prospector's terms for good measure. He wouldn't have been the first outsider to be hired by the mine, but he was the first to work for free, and the first to help the Coilhunter sneak inside.

Chapter Thirty-one

BOWLER BRONSON

The slaves wheeled the cart in. It was slow, and the wheels screeched against the tracks. They must've thought it was awful heavy with nothing in it, but then they were used to hauling heavy loads. Those who weren't used to it died. Those who got too used to it died as well.

Under the cover, Nox had to rely on different cues to tell him where he was. The darkness intensified, and he knew they'd passed through the door into the mine. He heard the far-off ping of pickaxes, the shuffle of worn-out feet, the heaving and panting of the slaves, the shouts of the mine captains, and the lash of their whips.

It took a lot of restraint for Nox to not leap out there and then and gun down those slave-drivers, or to put a shackle around their necks and make them dig their own six-foot mine. Some said all bad men were equal, but Nox didn't see it like that at all. There were shades of bad, and slavers were some of the worst.

"Faster!" a mine captain barked. "The ore is pilin' up down there!" He lashed his whip, and another man cried. It was one of the men pushing the cart.

They pushed it faster now.

Nox felt the cart dip, and he slid down an inch inside, his boots pressing against the end. The cover moved, and a fold formed that revealed part of Nox's face. A surprised slave stared at him. Nox held his index finger to his mask.

They pushed him on, down another slope, around several corners, deeper into the mine. They travelled past the shouts of many more slave-drivers, past their lashing whips, past the screams of several shades of good men.

Then the cart halted suddenly, and he heard the voice of Bowler Bronson. He knew it was his, because he could see that short, rotund chief through a gap in the cover, with his iconic hat and the smug smile of someone who'd gotten to where he was by climbing the backs of his fellows. And he was a whole iron cart of his own.

"Fill this up!" he roared, resting his fat fingers on his belly. "How're we gonna expand to the new mines if we can't even run this one properly. Time is coils, men! Coils!"

Bronson hobbled over to the cart and reefed the cover off. There, with twin pistols raised, was Nox, and you could tell he was smiling.

"Howdy," Nox rasped.

Bowler Bronson stumbled backwards in horror, barely even able to shriek.

Nox leapt up, landing his feet on either side of the cart. The guards didn't even have time to reach for their pistols before the Coilhunter gunned them down. That was the good part. The bad was that the slaves just stood there, trembling. They didn't even know that they could run.

"Get outta here!" Nox told them, and they went. Bronson tried to crawl away with them. "Not you," Nox added, standing on the back of his neck.

"Please!"

"I've been hearin' a lot of mannerless men discover manners lately," Nox said. He kicked Bronson onto his back. "It's just a pity they didn't discover 'em sooner." He drew in close, so that his mask almost pressed against Bronson's face. He breathed smoke into the man's eyes, so that the form of Nox he'd remember would be as ever-shifting as a nightmare.

"What do you want?" Bronson yelped.

"Answers," Nox said. "For now."

"Anything!"

It was a bad idea to say that. What if Nox wanted your life?

"You spoke to Honest Pete."

"I *had* to."

"Well," Nox croaked. "Now you have to speak to me."

Bronson trembled more than those slaves did. It was easy to be brave when you were holding the chains. Nox'd met a lot of brave men who flinched every time he moved. They might tell others they puffed their chests, but when the curtains moved in the middle of the night, they'd tremble.

"Who ordered you to tell Pete those lies?"

Bronson's eyes watered. "I can't. I can't say."

Nox breathed more of that black smoke his way.

"It wasn't personal, Nox. Honest!"

"Oh, it was personal to me. Now, you tell me quick, or I'll kill ya, and it'll be slow."

"That'll be nothin' compared to what *he*'d do. I'd rather die to you."

"Oh, don't you tempt the part o' me that'd rather kill ya."

"He'll destroy me, Nox."

"Not if I destroy him first. Now tell me, Bronson."

But Bronson refused to talk, so Nox had to show him that he could destroy him too. He dragged Bronson down one of the tunnels, shooting approaching guards as he went. He snuffed out lights as he passed, plunging them into almost total darkness. Then he came to a part of the tracks that looked like it approached an intersection.

"Dig," Nox barked to Bronson, kicking the knees from under him.

Bronson seemed confused. "But I have no shovel."

"You've got two hands," Nox said. "For now."

Bronson hesitated, but not for long. When Nox moved close, Bronson started digging frantically with his hands, right at the edge of the tracks.

"What're we diggin' for?"

"You'll see." He gave Bronson a little extra encouragement, pressing the butt of one of his pistols against the back of the man's neck. By rights he should've felt the lash of a whip.

Bronson dug around the tracks, then between them, until there was a passage just barely big enough to crawl into.

"Now," Nox said. "Get in."

"What?"

"Get in. Get under those tracks."

Bronson shook his head in confusion.

"This is your grave, Bronson. You better make sure it's comfy."

Bronson's trembles grew, but they weren't enough to break him yet. The trembles of the one he served seemed worse.

Nox forced Bronson to crawl beneath the tracks and squeeze into the shallow grave. It was so tight that his body pressed against the metal. His belly almost bulged through the tracks. Nox kicked the earth on either side into place, until there was no way out.

"He'll come for you," Bronson said.

"No," Nox replied. "I'm comin' for him."

"This won't change anything."

"Oh, it will for you."

Nox rested against the tunnel wall, folding his arms and pressing the sole of one foot against the wall. Bronson was trying to show his bravery, but Nox knew that wouldn't last. All it'd take was time.

Another cart appeared around the corner, pushed by more slaves. They halted nervously before the track where Bronson was buried.

"Wait," he cried.

"No, you carry on," Nox said, gesturing them through.

They hesitated for a moment, then pushed the cart again, right over Bronson. Nox could hear the man murmur assurances to himself. The slaves passed on, farther into the mine.

"You might as well kill me now, Nox!" Bronson shouted.

"No, I told you it'd be slow. You see, you're gonna die a natural death, right there beneath the tracks you make those slaves walk. They're gonna haul those carts, and you're gonna see the fruit of their labour. All that ore. All those coils just waitin' to be made. They're gonna walk across your face, Bronson. Every damn day they'll trod your body. But you won't die yet. No. You'll become part of the mine, just like they do, but you'll be part of it while you're still alive. Hell, they'll give you water, just enough to keep you breathin'. Maybe it'll be days. Maybe it'll be months. But it won't be quick."

Bronson's breathing was already heavy. The panic in him was rising. Nox waited a moment more for that man's thoughts to do the rest.

"Okay!" Bronson yelled. "Okay, okay. I'll tell you!"

"Go on."

"You get me outta here first."

"No, you tell me first."

"I want your promise," Bronson said, "that you'll let me free."

"I promise."

"On your honour, Nox."

"On my honour."

Bronson took a moment, burying the fear of the man he was about to name. "It was … it was …"

"You tell me now," Nox said, "before another cart comes by."

"It was Lawless Lyle."

Chapter Thirty-one

SEEIN' THE LIGHT

Lawless Lyle.

Nox knew that name. Everyone did. Some said the gang lords didn't answer to anyone, but they were wrong. They answered to Lyle. Everywhere the Coilhunter went, he found traces of Lyle's handiwork, undoing the good that Nox had done. Nox had a poster with Lyle's face on it, but Lyle had returned him the favour. He'd use what mattered most to the Coilhunter as his weapon: the law.

That name shouldn't have stung, but it did. It stung because Nox had tried to catch Lyle before, and failed. No one ratted him out. No one gave him in. The fear the Coilhunter had generated paled compared to the fear those who worked with Lyle felt. After the massacre of the tribal village, Nox could see why they felt it.

"Good," Nox said, reaching down to dig Bronson out.

"No," Bronson said. "It's *not* good. He'll know I told you."

"How'll he know? It could've been anyone who broke."

"Oh, he'll know. He always knows." Bronson

143

paused. "And no one breaks."

The Coilhunter hauled Bronson up to his unsteady feet. "*Everyone* breaks."

Nox forced Bronson to lead him out of the mine, up through the passage the iron-filled carts rolled. There were more guards along the way, but Nox took care of them easily. As they walked, the Coilhunter grilled Bronson on the whereabouts of Lawless Lyle.

"He'll be north-west of here, up near the Dry Dunes," Bronson revealed. He was a lot more talkative now. All you had to do was get the stopper out of the bottle. It didn't matter how much he poured. Lyle would kill him for the drop that contained his name.

"Why's he up there? There's nothin' there."

Bronson might've chuckled if he weren't so scared. "That's what men said about the land where this mine is now. Hell, that's what they said about the Wild North as a whole. It takes a man of imagination to come to the wastes and dig, and he'll be the man who then goes on to sell imagination to everybody else."

"So, Lawless Lyle is lookin' for more mines," Nox mused.

"He's lookin' hard," Bronson said. "He was hopin' you'd be outta the picture by the time he finds them."

"Well, you know what they say about hope in Altadas."

"I wish it wasn't true, because I hope you'll find Lyle, and I hope you'll kill 'im. If you don't, well, then I would've been better off under those tracks."

"You might still be, Bronson. You might still be."

They came to the end of the mine. Nox dragged

Bronson out in the blinding sunlight. They squinted and ducked beneath their hats.

Then, as Nox's eyes adjusted, he halted. There, ahead of him, was Chance Oakley, but he was kneeling, with both hands up in the air. Beside him stood a tribesman with no shirt, with warpaint on his face. His hair stood tall, with many feathers in it. Not least of all, he had a bow, with the string drawn, and an arrow pointed at Oakley's head.

Chapter Thirty-three

FLYING FEATHER

The tribesman stood resolute, puffing his chest. He wore a collar of animal fangs, the kind that came from the largest of beasts. His trousers were yellow and blue, and fringed down the side. His soft-soled shoes almost merged with the dirt. He carried a quiver on his back. Nox counted nine arrows. Plenty for all of them. This man was a bounty hunter of a different kind, the kind that wore his bounties.

The tribesman eyed Nox coldly, turning his attention to Bowler Bronson, who had a different kind of weapon pointed to his head.

"More killing," he said, shaking his head solemnly. "Let man go."

"No," Nox said. "He's a *bad* man."

The tribesman almost scoffed, though it didn't quite seem like he knew how. There was something wild about him, wilder than most. "You are bad man."

"No, I'm not, if you'll give me a chance to prove it."

"I don't think he believes in second chances," Oakley said, staring nervously at the tip of the arrow.

"Let land speak for you," the tribesman said.

Nox wasn't keen on that idea. The land wouldn't

have anything good to say.

"I'm just a poor miner," Bronson said, flinching dramatically from Nox. "He killed my men inside."

"Only the bad ones," Nox said. "And you haven't done a day's minin' in your life. You forced slaves to do it."

The tribesman wasn't buying it. By now, he'd heard of the slaughter in Ilouayisca, and heard that Nox was to blame.

"Let him go," he urged, nodding again to Bronson.

Nox gestured to Oakley. "Let *him* go."

"He is accomplice."

"Only recently," Oakley said, though that didn't help much.

"He's just a drifter," Nox said. "Let him go and I'll let this … this 'miner' go."

The tribesman paused for a moment, and you could see him thinking the matter over. He turned his head from side to side as he deliberated. Nox added that to his memory with the number of arrows.

"Okay," the tribesman said.

"On three."

"Hmm?"

"We let them go on the count of three."

"Why three?"

"The number doesn't matter!" Oakley said. "Can we just do this?"

Nox lowered his gun and let Bronson run away. Boy, he ran fast.

"Put your gun away," the tribesman said.

Nox complied, reluctantly. He kept his hand close enough that the draw would be quick. Oakley might fall, but Nox'd get his shot in before the tribesman pulled the second arrow.

"Go," the tribesman said to Oakley, but he kept his bow drawn.

Oakley got up slowly and backed away.

"Now, let's talk about the truth," Nox said.

"Truth is you killed many."

"Many, maybe, but not the ones you think."

"Land demands blood tribute."

"Umna was there. She saw. She knows I didn't do it."

"I know no Umna. Land is witness. Land is judge."

"You're not listenin'."

"I am not here to listen. I am Flying Feather, sent by Machu Muada, Mother-tribe. I am here to hunt. You are prey. Honour demands I give prey time to run. Then hunt begins. Land will give her judgement as you run."

Nox could see he wouldn't get through to this man. He was a hunter who wanted no bounty, who couldn't be influenced by coils. If honour drove him, then Nox had to find a way to prove that he was a man of honour. That meant finding the real killer.

But now he had to do it while he was prey.

Chapter Thirty-four

RACE IN THE WILDS

The Coilhunter ran, and Chance Oakley ran with him. They didn't know exactly how long Flying Feather would give them, but they knew there'd be trouble when that time ran out. Nox didn't want to have to kill a man over a misunderstanding. It certainly wouldn't help his reputation with the tribes.

They didn't need to dodge sentry bullets, because the sentries were fast asleep, with small darts protruding from their necks. It seemed that Flying Feather didn't just use arrows.

They found their steeds on the overlook and saddled up swiftly. Oakley's horse whinnied and Nox's monowheel rumbled. From this vantage point they could see their hunter sitting down cross-legged on the ground, communing with the land—with their apparent judge.

"Don't like the look o' him," Oakley said. But then he would say that when he'd just been looking at the man up the length of an arrow.

"Well, let's not keep lookin'," Nox replied. "We need to capture Lawless Lyle before our feathered friend captures us."

"Lawless Lyle, huh? That won't be easy."

Nox revved the engine. "Nothin' ever is."

They took off, down the hill and off north-west. Nox led, and Oakley's horse had trouble keeping up with the monowheel. Maybe he didn't entirely want to. That vehicle must've looked like the oddest of beasts. But then, so did Nox.

The Coilhunter flicked a switch on his monowheel, which set in motion two little brushes at the back of the vehicle. They swept over the tracks as they were made, helping to cover the trail. He couldn't do the same for Oakley's horse, but at least it might look like they split up. Normally Nox would let the shifting sands cover his tracks, or leave them for the criminals to see and fear. This time was different. This time he wasn't the hunter.

They drove on, dipping down dunes, crashing through the desert brush. There was no sign of Flying Feather behind them, and no suggestion that he had any steed of his own. Only the Losa Ariasa, the Dust Riders, rode horses, and Flying Feather had indicated that he was from the Mother-tribe. That didn't make Nox drive any slower. He wanted Lawless Lyle as much as he wanted to flee from arrow and dart.

And then the first sign came. It was the screech of a hawk, high up, following their trail. It didn't need to scour the sand for tracks. It could see them just fine.

Oakley took his rifle and aimed it at the bird. Nox had to swerve close to Oakley's horse to put him off the shot. The bullet cruised by the hawk.

"It's tracking us!" Oakley said.

"If that's Flying Feather's pet," Nox shouted over the sound of his engine, "then the last thing we need to do is kill it."

Oakley raised an eyebrow, but he put down his gun. Maybe he thought this would be his ghost's regret.

But Nox had a plan for the hawk. He bashed a few buttons on his wristpad, which beeped in response. Then he drove on, faster, leaving things to the wild. The hawk flew lower, until they could hear the wind sweeping through its wings, and its periodic high-pitched cries. It was almost as if it planned to attack.

Then there was a different sound, another cry, but it did not sound like any bird born of nature. Far off, from the direction of Canyon Crescent, came a mechanical owl, thundering through the wind as if it had been shot, not by a bow, but by a cannon.

The hawk saw it and swerved, trying to regain some height. The owl came down upon it, and they flapped and fluttered at each other, snapping and clawing. They tumbled through the sky, falling down into the dust hills ahead.

Nox might've smiled at this initial victory, were it not for the sweeping sandstorm that appeared ahead as they crested the next dune. The birds vanished into the haze, and Nox and Oakley would soon follow. The sand seemed to roll towards them, like a boulder of a million grains.

Then, from the centre of its depths, came an arrow.

Chapter Thirty-five

SANDSWEPT

The arrow struck Nox in the arm, and it struck hard. The force of it pushed him back, yanking his hand on the steering wheel. The monowheel swerved sharply, toppling onto its side. Nox rolled out, narrowly missing the top of the outer wheel as it fell.

Nox snapped the arrow, leaving the tip of it in to stop his blood gushing out. He didn't have the time to tend to his wounds. He had to stop himself getting any more.

The sand came in sudden and fast, lashing at his eyes. He pulled his hat down, then crawled towards the monowheel, patting the ground as he went. Nox fumbled with the panels on the monowheel, pulling out his goggles. They didn't help his vision much, because the wind coated them in sand as well.

He heard the frantic whinnies of Oakley's horse, along with the muffled cries of "There, boy, there!" Even now, in the midst of a storm of sand and battle, that old coot thought of Old Reliable.

"Get off the horse!" Nox shouted. The steed's braying only told the hunter where they were. Nox heard Oakley's same calming remarks to the horse.

"Get off!"

He had to pull him down, and he did it just in time. Another arrow sailed by, grazing the saddle.

"My horse!" Oakley cried as it rode off without him. Maybe it knew it wouldn't have a master to ride it soon enough.

The wind whistled sharply, and Nox dove to the ground, avoiding the next arrow that came his way. He lost his bearings in the tumble, with no visual cues for east or west. He tapped the buttons on his wristpad blindly, which started up the monowheel behind him. The wheel spun aimlessly on its side, kicking up more dust for the storm. It started up the fallen mechanical owl as well, which rose up and hovered in the air, shining its two headlight eyes into the haze.

The light helped a little, just enough to see a fleeting figure in the momentary breaks in the flurry of sand. The wind pushed against Nox, making his boots slide in the sand. He had to shoulder up against the invisible wall to stop from tumbling over.

Another arrow pinged, but this time it went for the owl, blasting through one of its shining eyes. It fluttered awkwardly. Then another came, taking out the other eye, and gloom returned to the sandshroud. Yet in the moment of those shots, Nox had wiped his goggles, and had caught a glimpse of Flying Feather just yards away.

He ran, straight for the tribesman, creating a channel through the dust as he charged. The next arrow came, skinning the Coilhunter's shoulder. Then Nox saw his target, readying the bow for another shot.

Nox flexed his right arm forward, fast and sudden, punching the wind. It triggered the grapnel launcher, which sent that metal hook out like an arrow of its own. Flying Feather wasn't ready for it, and the hook struck him square in the face, causing him to drop his arrow and stumble backwards, his head bobbing, his eyes blinking dumbly.

Nox kept going, even as the wind crowded in again, casting them back into a murky gloom. He stomped down on the fallen arrow, snapping it in two. Then he grasped at the empty air before him, casting a jab at the sheets of sand. He kept moving forward, until he tripped over Flying Feather, who had stumbled to the ground. They scrambled in the dirt for a moment, their limbs flailing, hitting nothing one moment, then each other, then an outcropping rock on the ground.

Nox used his fists in the frenzy, hoping not to have to use his gun. He thumped and bashed, and for a moment he thought he felt a moustache on the face he'd just then clobbered. He heard Oakley's moans, but couldn't place him. None of them knew who they were fighting, just that they had to fight.

"Stay back, Chance!" Nox called out, though his fist had probably told him enough. "You leave this to me."

But Chance Oakley didn't have much of a choice. Flying Feather took a blowpipe from his belt and spat a sleep-inducing dart at the drifter. Oakley went down quick, trying one vain swipe at the air before him.

Nox advanced, kicking the blowpipe from the

tribesman's hand. Then he heard the creak of a drawing string, and he would've taken his knife to cut it if he didn't worry he might stab Flying Feather instead. He grabbed at where he heard the sound, flinching as he felt the tip of the arrow when it moved into place. He didn't try to yank it free or block the strike. He just followed the line of it with his fist towards Flying Feather's jaw. The arrow pinged free, piercing nothing but the roiling sand.

Flying Feather punched back hard, growling as he struck Nox's mask. He got two hard hits into the Coilhunter's stomach, right where the wound was still far too fresh. Nox grunted and coughed. Then he felt a tug at his belt, and he realised that the tribesman was trying to take one of his pistols. Nox grabbed at the pawing hand, which unbuttoned the strap on his left holster. The gun inched in and out of its case, until Nox struck Flying Feather hard in the ear. That loosened the man's grip, just enough for Nox to take his pistol and cast it away into the sand. If he couldn't fire it, it was just another bow and arrow for his enemy.

In the flurry of it all, Nox didn't reach for his weapons. He threw them away. He cast aside his knives and threw away his guns. He cast aside his entire belt of gadgets. He was trying not to kill his enemy, and trying not to get killed by his own weapons. Most of all, he was trying to prove to Flying Feather that he wasn't an enemy, that he was an honourable man. He might as well've cast away his life.

The sandstorm passed, and the haze lifted. It revealed Flying Feather, standing at point blank range, with an arrow pointing straight at the Coilhunter's head. It revealed Chance Oakley dozing nearby. It revealed the Coilhunter with no weapons. A pistol lay mere feet away. He'd never reach it before the arrow pierced his skull.

Nox looked up at Flying Feather's bruised and bloodied face.

"It doesn't have to be this way," he said.

"It does," the tribesman said, and fired.

Chapter Thirty-six

THE LAST ARROW

The arrow stung like nothing else, throwing Nox back onto the ground. He grabbed his wounded shoulder, feeling the arrow deep inside. At the last moment, at the final second, Flying Feather had shifted his aim. Maybe it was his conscience speaking. Maybe it was the land. Something made him pause, and by the look of confusion on his face, even he didn't quite understand it.

Nox realised he'd been given an extra breath of life, and he didn't intend to use it to plead his case again. He'd tried the path of fists and the path of talking. Now it was time to try the path of pistols again.

He rolled onto his side, miming agony. He didn't have to do much acting. Then he made a frantic crawl for his pistol, grasping it even as Flying Feather reached for his quiver. The moment passed like forever, the tale of who reached the trigger first.

Flying Feather did.

But he was out.

Nox smiled, even through the pain. "What, you don't count your shots?"

"To count is to distrust land. So long as I trust

land, land provides."

"Well, it ain't provided now."

"Your blood shall water land. Your body will be soil."

"Sure, give it time. Hell, won't we all?" Then Nox clicked the hammer of his gun. "But here, let's water it together." He fired.

Flying Feather grunted as the bullet struck him in the shin, knocking him to his knees. A lone feather rocked on the wind nearby.

"Now," Nox said, forcing himself up. "You could say I wasted that shot. I could've put it in your chest or right between your eyes."

"I could have done same for you."

"And ya didn't, so I didn't. But I still can. Ya see, I count my shots, and I counted one left. Now, what I do with that one is up to you."

Flying Feather paused. He looked at his fallen bow. Then he sat back on his heels and placed his hands on his lap. He closed his eyes and bowed his head.

"What're ya doin'?" Nox rasped.

"I am asking land."

"Well, I didn't ask the land. I asked you."

"I serve land. Land must answer."

To some, that was madness. If Nox hadn't lived so long in the Wild North, he would've thought it was madness too. But he knew that the land wasn't just where you walked. It was a living, breathing thing, with sand in its lungs. Nox didn't have its ear, and didn't have his own to hear its voice. He'd tried the vision powder. He'd tried the journey tea. That just wasn't his path or his connection. His was the path alone, with his connection being the unwavering principles of the law.

He let Flying Feather commune with the land, wondering if the land would show its usual hatred of the Coilhunter, if it'd tell the tribesman that Nox had to die. Most of all, he wondered if he'd have to kill Flying Feather, if he'd have to become the lawless killer they all said he was.

In time, Flying Feather spoke, and his voice wavered. "Land is hurting."

There it is, Nox thought. *The land's death sentence.* At this stage, it could've been for both of them. Maybe Chance Oakley would wake up and have to drift solo.

But the look in Flying Feather's face had changed. The anger wasn't there, behind the puffy eyes and busted nose. Instead, there was worry.

"I didn't hurt the land," Nox said. He felt he'd have to make another case against another crime he didn't commit.

"No," Flying Feather said, stressing the word. "No, I know."

Nox gave him a moment.

"It is someone else."

"I told you that before," Nox said.

Flying Feather was about to answer, but he stopped short. Nox caught the tribesman's eyes focusing on something else, something far behind the Coilhunter.

They heard a sudden growl, and turned. There, coming over the dune, was Umna and her wolf, coming to answer the plight of the land, returning to join the hunt.

Chapter Thirty-seven

TROUBLED TERRITORY

It took some time to wake Chance Oakley, even with Flying Feather's smelling salts. It took longer for Nox to recover his weapons and tools, which the wind had tried to steal, and which the sand was trying to hoard. It took Umna no time at all to explain her journey, because she was a woman of few words.

"I followed the trail," she said.

"Was it that obvious?" Nox asked.

"When men tumble down dunes like children … yes."

"Did you find those stones?"

"Yes, but it wasn't easy. The Dew Distributors have put a claim on that river."

Flying Feather grumbled, poking at his bullet wound with the tip of a feather. It seemed like an odd attempt to sew it up.

"They're puttin' a claim everywhere," Nox said, cleaning up his own. He cast the arrow-tip on the tribesman's pile of recovered arrows.

The wounded tribesman flapped his arm instinctively. "Dewmen, hmm. Machu Muada will take care of that."

Umna studied Flying Feather and Chance Oakley

for a moment. "Who are these?"

"Friends," Nox said. "I think."

"Well, I am, at least," Oakley said. He lifted his chin at Flying Feather, as if his pride was wounded. But then being forced to your knees at arrow-point and knocked out by dart would probably do that.

Umna helped Flying Feather to his feet. They both formed their hands into what looked like a kind of claw, then gestured three times with them beside their ears. Nox hadn't seen that before, but then the tribes didn't often welcome outsiders.

Umna bowed her head and covered her eyes. "I am honoured."

"What's happenin'?" Oakley asked.

Flying Feather thumped his chest with his right hand. "I too."

They spoke in their tongue for a moment, and Flying Feather looked to Nox and nodded. Nox hoped Umna was saying nice things. The last thing he needed was the land to change its mind.

"So?" Nox asked when their conversation ended.

"We are waywalkers," she said, "while the way leads to the killer."

"What's that mean?" Oakley asked.

"We will journey together," Flying Feather said.

"A posse, huh?"

"A pack," Nox said, as the wolf pup let out a timely howl.

Nox filled in the newer members of the pack on what he'd learned so far, and all minds fixed on Lawless Lyle. Umna, most of all, urged that they waste no time in catching him. Not that Nox was planning to. If he hadn't had so many people hunting him, he might've caught that killer already.

They headed off as soon as they could, mapping the quickest way to the Dry Dunes. It was a few miles off, and they didn't have steeds for everyone. Yet one steed returned shortly after the sandstorm fully cleared.

"I named you well," Oakley said, patting the horse. Old Reliable nudged its head playfully at the wolf pup.

"Your hawk," Nox said to Flying Feather. "Is he not comin'?"

"Do you see him?"

"No, but—"

"He is coming," the tribesman said with an odd smile.

Nox just hoped his mechanical owl hadn't done too much damage. The land might've said Nox was good, but the tribesman could still make up his own mind about that.

Before they even reached the Dry Dunes, they felt the rumbles. The sand shook as if it was in a prospector's pan. But the earth trembled at almost perfect intervals, so Nox knew this was no natural phenomenon. It was the work of men.

They walked and rode, keeping their own steady, slow pace, but they had to stop altogether when the next rumble came in order to keep their footing. The closer they got to those sandy hills, the more they heard and felt the agitation of the earth.

When they arrived, they saw that the outer dunes dipped into a flattened area, and even from this vantage point they could see more of these bowl-shaped scenes, going on almost to the horizon. The Dry Dunes were being flattened one by one, with a tremendous network of explosives operating the execution. They could see vehicles and huts strewn between the wires, with dynamite by the dozen delivered by a constant ant trail of trucks.

"This is evil," Flying Feather said. "Even worse than you walled-ones."

"It's the work of Lawless Lyle," Nox said.

"Well, Nox," Oakley said. "I guess it's high time that son of a gun faces the law."

Chapter Thirty-eight

TEETH AND BONES

Nox's pack descended into the sand bowl, making their way to the centre. They went down slowly, slow enough for the men below to see them, slow enough for the fear to form in their minds.

There were many men, and all of them had guns and grizzled features. The land was unkind to all, but it was harsher to some. These were the kind of men who cracked glasses by staring at them, who their mothers looked away from. These were the kind of men who were destined for crime, for a life behind the wide-brimmed hat and raised neckerchief.

And there, among them, was Lawless Lyle. Nox could spot him from a mile away, having brooded over his mugshot on many sleepless nights. Lyle's hair was long and black, braided together with little skulls. His long, black beard was knotted in a similar fashion. He wore a black cowboy hat, with a band of skulls around it. His clothes were black, and his belt buckle was a skull as well. If nothing else, at least he was uniform.

Beside Lyle rode another figure the Coilhunter hadn't seen or heard of before: Bones Harry. His hair was shaved tight, and his face was gaunt, so that it almost looked like a skull as well. His eyes bulged in his head, and seemed far too big for it. He had a manic stare. But what Nox noticed most was that he nibbled at a chicken wing, and there were the discarded bones of many others in a pile nearby. It was a little detail, but it was the detail that had sealed his fate. Nox felt the anger rise in him, and it felt like the anger of more than one man. It felt the anger of a village.

Horseless mechanical wagons parked nearby, like the steam-powered warwagons used by the Iron Empire, except these were decorated more like the stagecoaches of old, painted black, with black curtains and a gold lace trim. They were a symbol of someone powerful, a vestige of the Treasury, now in the hands of the ones who used to rob them.

"Now, ain't that pretty," Lawless Lyle drawled. He smiled a long, broad smile, the kind that got under your skin. He looked at you like he knew he had you, like he had you all along. "The Coilhunter's got himself some friends. Whatever happened to bein' a lone wolf, Nox?"

"It's time to pay," Nox replied, holding up his pistol.

"Always talkin' coils," Lyle said with a laugh. "You should saddle up on this side, Nox. It's far more rewardin."

"There ain't nothin' rewardin' 'bout breakin' the law.

"We ain't got any place for law. This is the wilderness, Nox. This is the Wild North, God damn it!"

"Oh, he's damned it all right," Nox said. "And he's damned you as well."

Lyle sniggered. "And what's he done to you, Nox, huh? You think he's been good to you? If God does good things to good folk, then what does that make you?"

"Enough o' God-talk!" Chance Oakley bellowed. "This is about puttin' things right."

"This is about the law," Nox said.

Lyle enjoyed that, and it showed. "Ha! And look what I did to your precious law. You're the law, and those folks huntin' you are the law. Hell, I'm the law now too. I made a mockery outta you, Nox."

The smoke blasted out of Nox's mask. "Just wait till you see what I make outta you."

"You kill me and this whole thing'll come tumblin' down. I'm the centre of it all, holdin' it all together."

Nox clicked the hammer. "Then maybe it should fall."

"You think it's bad now?" Lyle asked. "I'm the monster keepin' all the other monsters at bay."

"But you're still a monster."

"Give it time, law-boy. Give it time. You'll be one o' us too."

Lawless Lyle didn't know it, but Nox was already concerned about just how much he'd driven him to the edge. He'd almost destroyed the core of him, turning him into what he'd hunted, blurring the line between predator and prey. Lyle was the king of his own criminal jungle, roaring at the animal in everyone. Some of them roared back, and Nox's inner beast had almost joined them. But he kept it locked up, and kept the hatches down. He told that beast that he was the boss of it. If you could tame that, well, then maybe you could tame the wild.

"What you did back in Ilouayisca was evil," Nox said. "Many dozen evils."

Lyle shrugged. "Was it? Oh, I'm glad you told me." He slapped his hand. "No more o' that, now." He laughed boisterously, and the others laughed with him. Nox knew they wouldn't think it was funny in a moment.

Bones Harry spit a bone right at the Coilhunter. "Was that the village with the savages?"

Flying Feather shifted his feet in the sand. Umna stared with the eyes of many.

"You know, Nox," Lyle said. "We lured those men up the mountain like animals."

"Slaughtered 'em like animals too," Harry said, spitting out another bone.

"And what we did to the *women*," Lyle added with a smile. "Well, Nox, you're a man with a mind. And maybe you're a man with needs too." Lyle paused and grinned. "Well, that whole damn village didn't meet mine."

The laughter erupted again like gunfire. Far off, the earth rumbled.

"You can come quietly," Nox said, "and tell Hardwell the truth."

"Or?" Lyle said, wagging his tongue at the Coilhunter.

"We can do this the old-fashioned way."

"Well, call me traditional then. Let's decide who walks, who limps, and who don't move at all."

They squared off with their eyes. They dug their heels into the sand. They dangled their trigger fingers.

They waited for the silent countdown in their minds.

And yet, in the moment of deciding, something else occurred.

They heard the rumble of engines. Half a dozen three-wheeled motorcycles came over the dune, and on them were propped many familiar bounty hunters: Sour-faced Saul, Iron Ike, Long-eyed Lizzy, and Gold-barrel Jane. There were two others Nox didn't recognise, but he recognised why they were here. The bounty on Nox's head was even higher now, and it was a sizeable sum even when split six ways.

"Give it up," Saul shouted. "You're surrounded."

Nox almost laughed, if it wasn't for the irritation of their arrival, and he wasn't prone to laughter. "Come back with all the Deadmakers first, Saul. That ain't much of a wall you've got there."

And then, as if on cue, others arrived. It wasn't the Deadmakers. It was almost everybody else. The Losa Ariasa—the Dust Riders—came upon their glorious gold-maned horses, emerging from what seemed like an ever-swirling shield of dust devils. Moments later, a gang of twenty bandits came on foot, some brandishing crude weapons, all of them brandishing black hearts.

The people gathered around the basin, eyes wild with the lust of the kill. The ghosts of Ilouayisca must've shivered. There at the Dry Dunes were all the ingredients of another massacre—except this time there were more guns.

Chapter Thirty-nine

STAND-OFF

Everyone eyed each other coldly, and they did it colder with the eyes of their guns. It was a stand-off, with far too many standing. But that's the thing about stand-offs—folk don't stay standing for long.

"Finally caught up with ya," Sour-faced Saul said. "You didn't really think you'd escape, did ya?"

Nox stared at him. "Well, I already did before."

"He's an innocent man," Oakley said. "It's these folk here that done it."

"That's what they all say."

"Well, this time," Nox said, "it's the truth."

"Land is witness," Flying Feather added. "Land agrees."

Umna nodded solemnly.

"What, little old me?" Lawless Lyle said.

"You just admitted it a minute ago," Oakley said.

"Admitted what?"

"No more o' your tricks, Nox!" Saul shouted. By now, this was more than just a bounty. It was personal. It's bad when a man thinks he's lucky, but it's worse when he thinks he's been cheated of luck.

The other bounty hunters all had their reasons too. They kept their rifles and pistols raised, but they all pointed at different targets. Some of them even recognised Lawless Lyle, though by now the bounty on Nox was higher than his. It was starting to look like maybe they could get a two-for-one deal in this battle.

Then the earth boomed.

"What's that?" Gold-barrel Jane asked, shifting her gun around as if to shoot some invisible bomber.

Lawless Lyle laughed. "That's the sound of industry, sweetheart, and it's gonna keep on soundin' after we're finished addin' our own gun chorus."

"It is sin against land," Flying Feather said.

Lyle cackled. "That just makes it all the better, bird-boy. It's sin that makes life worth livin'."

"Well," Nox rasped, "you better do all your sinnin' right here and now, because you ain't gonna live much longer."

The Dust Riders chanted from the dunes. It was a slow chant, but it started to gain speed quick.

"I don't like the sound of that," Oakley said.

Flying Feather bobbed to the tune. "Ride to war."

"A battle cry," Umna added.

"The problem is," Nox said, "I think we're all their enemies."

Flying Feather said nothing, perhaps to avoid having to agree.

Then the earth rumbled. They heard the far-off boom of dynamite.

"Put it down, Nox," Gold-barrel Jane urged. She was the newest of the Deadmakers, always trying to prove herself, and never really being accepted by them. Some said she'd rebelled against the Treasury, and that was where she got her gun, but it was a dangerous thing to target Nox in your rebellion. You couldn't prove yourself if you were dead.

"I'll take my chances with you," Nox replied. "You're a gambler to use that gun."

And she was, because Jane's gold-barrel gun was an ancient relic, a Treasury display pistol that Jane used as her signature piece. It was made to look good, and Jane picked it to look good too. With so many menacing figures in the Wild North, with memorable names and gimmicks, she needed to stand out from the pack. Having a gun that jammed nine times out of ten would do it, but it was the wrong way to stand out. Hell, she was lucky she was still standing.

"I don't want to kill you, Nox," Jane said. Her voice made that clear. All she wanted was recognition. Well, Nox recognised her now. Maybe, if she kept going this route, she'd have her own poster too. Everyone would recognise her then.

"Don't you worry, Jane," Nox rasped. "You won't."

Then the earth rocked. They struggled with their footing.

The bandits began their own chant, but it was chaotic, just like their crude collection of weapons. Some of them had guns and some of them had machetes and flails. Maybe if they got the Coilhunter's head back to the Bounty Booth, they could afford something better. Nox saw them as a mere distraction, but they were a dangerous one.

As guns moved from target to target, and other guns moved in response, and all eyes darted back and forward, and all feet moved to and fro, it seemed like everyone was locked together. One man prevented another from shooting. A temporary truce was secured by the complex web of war.

Throughout all this, Bones Harry never even drew his gun. He kept on chewing his chicken wings, flinging away another bone. He'd killed so many before that he assumed this would be no different. And he always ate before the battle. Everyone was almost waiting for the final bone.

Then the earth quaked. The rumbles were closer than ever, and ripples formed within the sand.

"Well, Nox?" Lawless Lyle asked. "Who's gonna fire first?"

Nox didn't reply. He was more concerned about who fired last, who survived all this. It wasn't just him he had to worry about. It was why he usually liked to do things alone.

All hands that weren't already holding a gun hovered at their hips. All eyes locked on their targets. All boots shifted subtly in the sand. All minds readied for the draw and the kill.

The earth quaked again, but this time more violently than before. Just as the silent countdown of the stand-off reached zero, the ground erupted suddenly, tossing the gunslingers and bandits and bounty hunters in all directions. Great chasms formed in the sand, and from those chasms came enormous, flesh-devouring sandworms.

Chapter Forty

WORMS FOR THE LIVING

The worms varied in height and size, but all of them were at least twice the height of men, and with bodies that spanned ten to twenty metres in length. Their skin was tan, but their markings were different. Some had ridges down their spines. Others had horns on their heads. All of them had great, gaping mouths, with many rows of razor-sharp teeth.

And they were hungry.

And they were angry.

The booms brought them. The booms awakened them. The booms opened up the underground caverns and chambers where they burrowed, slept and bred. Now they came above ground to fight and feast.

Almost simultaneously, the worms rose up to their full height, bending their bodies, and then swung back down with their maws wide, devouring in one go anyone who was close enough to catch. Two bandits were consumed. Four of Lyle's men were gobbled up. A Dust Rider was swallowed, horse and all. Sour-faced Saul's bike was gulped down after he leapt from it just in time.

Then the guns fired like a battery of cannons. The

gunpowder made its own dust clouds. The worms roared as everyone turned their weapons upon them, unified in this moment when the land suddenly took on them all.

But the bullets only made the sandworms more enraged. The gunners gave them metal, but they really wanted flesh. The more their hide was pierced and slashed, the more they wriggled and writhed, and the more they turned their snarling maws upon the banquet of men.

The Dust Riders charged, kicking up the sand into a swirl. The wind lashed at the skin of the sandworms, and the Losa Ariasa followed with the lash of their blades. Their horses danced in and out of their sandshroud, and the riders bellowed a terrible war cry to match the ear-rending roar and wail of the worms.

One of the sandworms coiled around a Dust Rider, corralling the horse within the bulk of its form. The rider fired everything he had, and the horse bucked and kicked. Then the worm squeezed tighter, until the shrieks and yelps faded into nothing. It devoured the remains.

The sight of this sent many of the Ootana-bred horses of the Losa Ariasa reeling. They turned on the spot, and their frantic brays drowned out even the shouts and calls of their masters. Some threw their riders, others rose up to threaten the worms with their front legs, and others galloped from the battlefield in a trail of dust.

But one horse didn't buck or flee. It was Old Reliable, which Chance Oakley rode into the fray. He hung on with his legs, for in one arm he carried his rifle, and in the other a rope, which he swung around the neck of one of the approaching worms. It fell into place, and he tugged and fired. But it tugged back, yanking him from his saddle. He tumbled in the dirt, and the worm rose high above him, ready to gulp him down.

It was then that the Coilhunter rode by, parking the monowheel like a shield in front of Oakley. The worm's head came down, and its mouth latched onto the top of the outer wheel, but it couldn't get its jaw around it all. Nox spun the wheel ferociously, tearing through the teeth of the creature, and he fired round after round of his shotgun straight into the gullet of the beast. It roared and moaned, then reared its head again before slumping dead to the ground.

"Thanks," Oakley said, as Nox helped him to his feet.

"Thank me later if you're still alive."

Nox tossed him another rifle, then blasted off again, zig-zagging between battles, casting gadgets from his belt and bullets from his guns.

Suddenly the ground burst again, and out of it came dozens of smaller sandworms, about the size of a human arm. They scurried across the sand in all directions, slurping up whatever was left by their larger kin.

Umna raced back up the slope, turning to fire her rifle at the smaller worms that followed. Her wolf pup ran between her legs, then leapt from one approaching worm to another, snapping at their necks, tearing at their hide with his claws.

Flying Feather leapt into the air. In a sudden flurry that defied sight, he transformed into the hawk that had chased Nox across the wilds. Feathers exploded outwards, masking the transformation, and the hawk rose high into the sky, far above the rampage of the worms. It was there, while the sun glistened on its beak and the wind rustled through its wings, that the transformation occurred again, and he was suddenly a man once more, still leaping, but now poised in the sky with bow drawn. He fired, and just as the arrow left the bow, he changed into a bird again, halting his fall.

Flying Feather soared above the battle, taking out one of the larger worms with every arrow he had left. But it wasn't worms that bird hunted. It was the men who summoned them. He dove down towards Lyle's men, shifting back into a man in time to seize one of the figures, wrapping his arm around the man's throat. He squeezed tight and dragged the criminal back on his heels. The struggle sent up sand and feathers. Then the struggle ended, and the worms had one more prepared feast.

He continued through Lyle's men, shifting forms, flapping his wings madly in their faces, scratching at their eyes. Then, as a man again, he choked them, and he might have done more if he didn't need to choke others. When one man came to the aid of another, he shifted back into a bird, reducing his body mass to avoid the incoming bullets. Throughout the battle, he flew and walked and ran, but most of all he killed. And the land was happy.

Gold-barrel Jane struggled with her gimmick

gun. The smaller worms swarmed her as she backed away. She clicked the trigger. It jammed. She clicked again. It croaked. A worm slithered up her boot and she kicked it away. She fiddled frantically with the safety. She probed desperately at the chamber. Then she got one shot off, blasting one of the worms apart. But more came, and her gun betrayed her again.

Yet even as they came, Umna turned her gun from her own plight to Jane's, taking down each worm that crawled and coiled its way up the young bounty hunter's body. When Jane opened her eyes again, she blinked at the tribeswoman standing across the way, standing on what was the enemy's side only moments before. Jane tried to say her thanks, but Umna already turned back to the battle. If Umna was a talkative type, she might've said: *You can say your thanks by living*.

Through the screams and the clatter of gunfire, Lawless Lyle and Bones Harry tried to flee. They let loose their initial rounds, but they quickly abandoned the fight, leaving it to their men and the others. They clambered into their separate wagons, firing them up with frenzied shovelfuls of coal. The steam engines spluttered and the vehicles rolled away.

Chapter Forty-one

WORMS FOR THE DEAD

The wagons thundered off, heading for safety outside the Dry Dunes. They started together, but soon split up when the worms pursued them. Nox also followed swiftly.

Lyle's wagon turned sharply, rocking onto one side, then coasted the body of the largest worm. Every time a path opened up, it closed just as suddenly, with the rearing head of a worm slamming down into the sand.

The Coilhunter marked Lawless Lyle's wagon in his mind, spotting the small differences between the two: the extra wearing on the wheels, the closed curtains, the small scratch on the back. He kept those features in his mind like he kept the ones of the faces he hunted.

But every predator is its own prey, and hot on the heels of Nox came Sour-faced Saul, riding on the back of a motorcycle with Long-eyed Lizzy. She rode hard, and he balanced himself on the back with a rifle in each hand. He fired at Nox, clipping at the wheel, punching a little hole in the fuel tank. The diesel leaked out, and Saul cast a match at it as he passed, so that even the fire chased the Coilhunter.

Then, as Lizzy's bike got close—close enough for her short-sightedness to see—Gold-barrel Jane came in from the side on her own bike and rammed them.

"Jane!" Saul cried. "What're you doin'?"

Jane answered with another swerve, smashing the wheels together.

"You'll be out of the Deadmakers!" Saul warned.

And maybe that was true, but if Saul died, he would be as well.

Jane bashed her bike against theirs once more, knocking it to the side. Long-eyed Lizzy lost control, and her and Saul rolled off into the flames they'd formed. They roared and ran, rolling around in the sand like worms of their own.

Nox looked back at Gold-barrel Jane, who nodded to him. He nodded back, then returned his attention to Lawless Lyle. The wagon wasn't as agile, but it was far ahead of the Coilhunter's monowheel. Lyle must've known that Nox was on his trail, because he took bigger risks. He almost plunged straight into the mouth of a worm, hoping that it would snatch up his pursuer instead. Another worm crashed down nearby, sending the wagon rocking. It skidded to a halt.

Nox pressed hard on the accelerator. Even from there he could see Lyle's evil eyes and his manic grin inside the wagon. Lyle didn't show fear like the others. He enjoyed the chase, the hunt. Most of all he enjoyed making the Coilhunter struggle and suffer. If he was to go down, he wouldn't go down easy.

And yet down was where he went. He powered up again, throwing more coal on the fire. When he sped off, he didn't just cross the bumpy sand. He dipped down into one of the tunnels the giant worms came from. It was madness to go down there, it seemed, but then it was madness to stay above as well. So he went, deep into the pits of the earth.

And Nox followed.

Harry's wagon reached the edge of the basin, but its wheels jammed in the sand, spinning wildly, kicking up a dust storm that attracted the attention of many of the worms that had previously assailed Umna. When she saw where they were going, she stopped firing. It would be fitting if creatures of the earth took Bones Harry.

Harry reached out of the window of his wagon with a shovel, stretching down to scoop wildly at the wheels. The wagon inched forward a little, then jammed again. And as Harry shovelled madly, the worms came. He smacked one with the shovel and sliced another in half with the blade. But more came, and he was forced to switch to his pistols. They slithered up the wagon, coiling around the wheels, until Harry knocked them off with bullet and boot.

He was alone in his wagon, having been selfish enough to not take anyone with him. So, he was alone in fighting off the swarm. As soon as he cleared one side, he had to race to the other, for the worms were dropping in through the window there. The screams and gunfire sounded for a long time, and then Bones Harry no longer appeared at the windows. More worms congregated, filling up the inside of the wagon, almost bursting through its hull.

They devoured Harry, taking tiny bits of him at

a time. He was alive for it all. They nibbled away his fingers, so he could no longer shoot. Then they took his limbs, so he couldn't fight. Then they took the rest of him.

All they left was the bones.

Chapter Forty-two

TUNNELS

Nox pursued Lawless Lyle into the tunnels. There were steep slopes, up and down, and many winding bends, but the monowheel could handle it. Lyle's wagon couldn't handle it quite as well, clattering off the walls and bouncing over ridges. It made a constant clang, like a homage to the boomsticks above. Nox only hoped it wouldn't awaken anything else.

They travelled the network of tunnels, which could've gone anywhere, but most of all they seemed to go down deeper underground, into the grave of the earth, to where Lawless Lyle doubtless belonged. But it could've been anyone's grave. There was time yet for it to be the Coilhunter's too.

They passed by a large cavern, packed with the eggs and larvae of dozens more sandworms. Some of them were already hatching, devouring their nearby siblings. It wouldn't take them long to grow to the size of their parents. This was all the work of nature, but no one ever said that nature was nice.

Farther on, they passed through a tunnel of glimmering stones, and then another with veins of gold. In a different time, these would've been the find of finds, but in the time of the Iron Empire they were mere decoration. Lawless Lyle paid them no heed at all.

Suddenly the wagon seemed to vanish, except for the clatter of its bonnet off a wall, and the rev of its engine, and the constant spinning of its wheels. Nox slowed, then came to a halt at the edge of a deep chasm in the tunnel, which seemed to go down into an eternal darkness. No, maybe *that* was where Lawless Lyle belonged.

The wagon was stuck several metres down, wedged diagonally against the two opposing walls. Lyle hung upside down by his foot, caught by one of the straps that previously held the dynamite in place. He tried in vain to pull himself up.

Nox sauntered to the edge and threw a lit match down. It fluttered past Lyle's face and seemed to go on forever, until the darkness consumed it.

"Well, now," Nox rasped.

"Sorry, Nox. I can't hear you. Why don't you jump down here and say it again?"

Even now, Lyle taunted him. Even in defeat, he acted like he'd won.

The wagon creaked, then slipped down another foot. Lyle yelped, then caught his breath as the vehicle lodged in place again. It groaned loudly.

"So, this is how I go," Lyle said, looking down into the gloom.

"No," Nox said. "That ain't how you go."

The wagon slipped again, as if to prove him wrong. But Nox hadn't pictured it ending like this. He promised Umna she could have the honour, no matter how much he wanted to do it himself. He intended to keep that promise.

Lyle knew it. He could clearly see the determination in the Coilhunter's eyes. And because he was Lawless Lyle, he just couldn't give Nox the satisfaction. So, he took a knife from his belt and held it aloft.

"Wanna bet?" he said.

Nox jumped down, even as Lyle stretched up and started sawing at the strap. Nox landed on the roof of the wagon, which caused it to plummet another foot, almost throwing him off. Lyle was halfway through the strap by now.

And then, as Nox clambered around the side of the vehicle, the strap broke and the knife tumbled from Lyle's hand. Lawless Lyle gave a smile that would've haunted Nox for the rest of his life, the smile of one final victory, were it not for the fact that Nox had grasped Lyle's ankle right at the last moment.

"Let me go!" Lyle shouted.

"No one escapes the law!" Nox shouted back.

Lyle reached up, trying to uncurl Nox's clenched fingers—but Nox held tight. No matter how much Lyle weighed, no matter how much his muscles strained, no matter how much the wound in his gut gnawed at him. Each time they tried to weaken him, he just held on tighter. He tried to haul Lyle up, but gravity was also in this fight, and it was a reigning champion.

Then the wagon gave what sounded like its final death throes. The rock crumbled away on either side. It was clear that the next time, it wouldn't catch in place.

"Let's go together then," Lyle said, giving once again that haunting smile.

The wagon fell, and Nox fell, and Lyle fell, into the gloom together.

Chapter Forty-three

THE LAWLESS AND THE LAW

Nox plummeted, but even then he wouldn't let go of Lyle. If he had to, he'd go to the grave with him, the lawless and the law. He'd bring justice to the frontiers of the afterlife.

But the Coilhunter knew he could still do justice in this one.

He fired a grappling hook up, barely seeing where it went, trusting that the land which Lyle had hurt would reach out its outcropping limbs. It caught in place high above, and the tug loosened Nox's grip on Lyle.

The wagon tumbled past them, and they didn't hear its final crash below. Lyle's smile faded. He hadn't yet learned the truth about the Coilhunter, that even if Lyle hid in Hell, Nox would stroll through the flames to drag him out.

They rose slowly as the wire recoiled. It took every ounce of Nox's strength to keep a hold of Lyle. Every muscle bulged. Every sinew screamed.

When they reached the top again, they found Umna there with her wolf pup, waiting—waiting for that promise to be fulfilled. She helped pull Nox and Lyle in. The wolf pup tried to help too, biting at Lyle's trouser leg.

"So," Lyle said, panting. "That's not how it ends."

"No," Nox said. "Not for you."

"Y'know, some old hag from the savages told me she saw how I was gonna die," Lyle mused. "I told her hers with my gun."

"How do we do this?" Umna asked Nox.

"Want me to tell you what she said?" Lyle asked.

"I need a moment with him," Nox said, "and then he's yours."

"She said I'd die by my own hand," Lyle said, laughing. "For a moment there in that hole, I thought I would."

"You do die by your own hand," Umna said. "It was your actions, your evil deeds, that doomed you. Whatever death you have, you were what birthed it."

"You could say that for all men," Lyle responded, "and all women."

"No," Umna said, shaking her head slowly. "Many died a death that you made. They didn't create it. Nothing they did made them deserve it. But you … you deserve every death. I just wish … I just wish I could give you them all."

Nox stepped closer to Lyle. "Well, we can give 'im one."

Chapter Forty-four

JUSTICE

Lawless Lyle tried to crawl away, liked he'd always tried to crawl away from the law. It was a sorry sight to see a grown man on his hands and knees, traipsing through the dirt like a child. Yet Lyle didn't have a child's innocence. He went and shot that too.

"You come back now," Nox said, striding after him. No matter how fast Lyle crawled, Nox's strides were faster. He caught him by the scruff of the neck and turned him round. Oh, he was a sorry sight indeed. Nox almost felt merciful.

Almost.

"You did a lot of evil in this world," Nox said.

Lyle's lip didn't utter any defence. He didn't care to justify his actions, because he didn't believe in justice. Well, he should've believed in Nox.

"I pity the next world that gets you."

"Please!" Lyle begged, but he did it sarcastically, feigning a sob. By the end of it, Nox hoped it'd be real.

"You better beg God," Nox said. "Why, you better beg the Devil." He wondered if Lyle would do it derisively then.

He dragged him on, dragging out the end. Lyle didn't deserve a slow death. There were far too many dead who needed to see him go. By rights, he deserved a hundred bullets, maybe more—if only Nox could make him last that long.

Lyle tried to grab the ground, to hug the ground, to clutch and cling to it for life, if for nothing more than to make it difficult for Nox. But the land wouldn't save him. It had decreed this end. As Umna would say, it was the way.

Nox turned Lyle onto his back and planted his boot on the man's heaving chest.

"You sullied my name," Nox said. "You did your evil and you put my name on it."

He drew in close, sighing out his black smoke, until the form of him was frightening.

"This is justice," Nox said. "Now spell it for me."

No one would've spelled that, and many didn't know how. But Nox drew the letters like he drew blood. Yet, when Lyle spoke those letters, he did it to taunt him, smiling all the way.

"J," he said.

"U." He puckered his lips at Nox in jest.

"S," he hissed, drawing it out, enjoying every moment of it.

No doubt he would have used each remaining letter to knife away at Nox's mind—if Nox had let him.

"No," the Coilhunter said, taking his dagger out. "You spell it N."

He carved the letter into Lyle's forehead.

"O."

Lyle screamed.

"X."

He dropped the criminal, letting the blood roll down into his eyes, until, when he looked at Nox through the blood and the smoke, he saw something red and black, and altogether harrowing. It was like he saw the Devil himself. Soon, he would.

"He's all yours," Nox said to Umna.

Umna strolled over and took a pebble from her pocket. Now, you'd think Lawless Lyle wouldn't deserve her blessing. She placed the stone on the man's chest, and he gawked at it in confusion. She didn't say much. The dead said it all.

"That stone's different," Nox said, noting the design etched upon it.

"I know."

Lyle picked it up. "What the hell is—?"

Umna fired her rifle. Lyle's arm dropped, still clutching the stone.

"Your blessing?" Nox asked.

Umna's face was placid. "My permission to die."

Chapter Forty-five

FLYING LOW

The battle was over, and the Dry Dunes were littered with the bodies of worms and men. The survivors patched themselves up, and the best of them patched others too.

Nox and Umna left the tunnels, dragging Lawless Lyle behind them. Chance Oakley was there, along with Flying Feather and Gold-barrel Jane.

"Sorry I didn't believe you," Jane said.

Nox tipped his hat. She'd already said sorry in the way that mattered.

"Land is at peace," Flying Feather said, almost smiling.

"Good," Nox said. He was too.

Nox sealed the hole on the engine of his monowheel and refilled the tank with the spare diesel canister. It'd get him home, at least. He looked at Lawless Lyle, sprawled in the bounty box at the back. It'd get him home too.

Nox rested on the seat of the monowheel, his arms crossed. He surveyed the battlefield, with its new dunes made of men and worms. The wind was already starting to bury them, that ever-respectful wind, which'd bury you while you were living.

"All this for a name," Oakley said, drawing up beside him with Old Reliable.

"Well," Nox said, "it's a good one."

Umna looked at him with a hint of sorrow in her eyes, which she buried just as quickly. It was one of the few things the wind wouldn't touch, so you had to do the digging yourself. Her look told the Coilhunter something very clear: *Your name. It's all you've got left.*

"Will it be enough?" Jane asked. "I mean, will this clear you of those crimes?"

"It'll have to."

"I can vouch for you, at least," Jane offered. It was certainly the least she could do, after trying to gun him down. But it was more than most would do. For some, it wouldn't matter if there was a poster or not. Nox was anathema to the wild and the lawless.

Nox nodded to her. He just hoped her word was more reliable than her gun.

"So," Nox said, looking Flying Feather up and down. "You're a shape-changer, huh? That's … new."

Flying Feather smiled. "Older than you walled-ones," he said. "You don't remember us, because you moved on to other things, like machines."

"I think I'd remember you," Nox said.

"You will now."

Nox didn't deny that. "So, how does it work?"

"Land will answer, if you ask land."

"Ah," Nox said. "One of those answers." All Nox knew was that if he listened close enough to the land, he could almost hear it say: *Give it time, Coilhunter. I'm already hunting you.*

* * *

It was good to rest a moment, to not always have a finger on the trigger, to even briefly fly under the radar. But in the Wild North, those moments come and go like gunfire. It didn't take long before Nox would have to add his own again.

"You," Sour-faced Saul growled from behind him.

Nox sighed. *Back to the grindstone*, he thought. Some folk just weren't going to let this go.

"Give it up," Nox said, not even bothering to turn. "You lost."

Saul had realised by now he wasn't lucky at all, and a wounded pride was an even more dangerous thing. Dangerous for others, and dangerous for himself. If your pride couldn't take those wounds, then maybe your body would.

"You still deserve to die," Saul said.

"Maybe I do," Nox rasped, "but it won't be you that does it."

But Saul had to push his luck, had to air his pride. Nox heard the shuffle of metal rubbing against leather as that bounty hunter pulled his pistol out of the holster. That was when Nox turned, grabbing his own in the process, and fired without even looking. All he needed was Saul's voice, and the knowledge that Saul always fired from the hip.

Saul yelped as he dropped his right pistol, but he had to push a little more, reaching for his left. Nox pinged that out of his hand too, and Saul got to keep his hands—and his life. Suppose he was lucky after all.

"One of these days," Saul said, pointing a quivering finger at him.

"What?" Nox asked. "You mean, one of these days I'll stop lettin' you go?"

Long-eyed Lizzy led Saul away, telling him it wasn't worth it, but casting a cold eye back at the Coilhunter in the process—a cold, human eye. Her mechanical one still needed the kind of repairs that only one like Nox could make. But her own wounded pride meant she'd never ask him. Nox's cold, calculating mind meant he'd never do it. He made dangerous toys, but not everyone got to play with them.

"One of these days!" Saul shouted back.

Yeah, Nox taught. *But not today*.

Chapter Forty-six

BACK TO THE BOOTH

Nox travelled back to the Bounty Booth, where they'd put up another poster with his face and name. Yet this time he didn't travel alone. Umna was there, stolid as ever. Chance Oakley was there, sucking another boiled candy. Flying Feather was there, with a few feathers less than before. Gold-barrel Jane was there, with a bit more experience under her belt.

They crowded the room with Hardwell, who didn't quite know who to look at. He looked at Nox, then back to the poster the Coilhunter'd torn down and slapped on the table.

"You hear their testimony, and then you order these to be taken down from every wall."

"I—"

"You hear their testimony," Nox said, stomping outside to haul a body in. "Or you hear his."

Hardwell looked over the counter to see Lawless Lyle on the floor, paler than ever. The colour suited him.

"I suppose you'll be wanting a reward," Hardwell said.

"No. I want my name back, and I want it back clean."

"That's up to the people."

"No, it ain't. It's up to you."

It was true that the people gave him the name Coilhunter, saying he hunted coils. That iron currency had the image of the Iron Emperor on one side, so some said that one day he'd hunt the Iron Emperor as well. It was a comment that wasn't lost on Hardwell and his kin.

Hardwell reluctantly listened to the accounts given by the four witnesses, before taking Nox's words. He wrote them all down and sent off his reports, along with his assessment that the Coilhunter was a law-abiding man. The accounts of the witnesses, including two tribespeople, and some of those who'd hunted Nox, helped seal the deal. If nothing else, the Iron Empire still felt the Coilhunter could be of some use. Nox always wondered how long that'd last.

Hardwell sent letters out to Regime territory, and to all the saloons across the Wild North. He told them to take down their posters. He took down his own ones of Nox, and those of Lawless Lyle as well. He cast them into the fire, that all-too-familiar fire. If you looked closely, you'd see Nox's face on the poster burning inside.

"They said he was unreachable," Hardwell said. "Lawless Lyle, that is."

"Well, there ain't anyone outside o' the reach of the law."

"Even you?"

"Even me."

"They feared him, you know," Hardwell said. "The other gangs."

"Don't you worry, Hardwell. They can fear me."

It was one of the few times he walked out of the Booth without a pocketful of coils. He'd made his living going in and out of there, but this time he walked out with just a lungful of air. It was worth many times more. And, more than anything, he still had his principles. His father used to tell him that you can't eat principles. And no, you couldn't. But you could live by them.

Chapter Forty-seven

FIVE WENT IN

The deed was done, and the Coilhunter's unlikely posse gathered outside the Bounty Booth, staring at the setting sun, as if even it had stopped chasing Nox.

"Well," Nox said. "I owe you all a debt I probably can't pay."

Umna stayed silent, Oakley removed his hat and smiled, Flying Feather bowed his head, and Jane shrugged her shoulders.

"I can't thank you enough," Nox said.

"So, what does this mean?" Jane asked. "Is this it?"

Flying Feather pulled a feather from his hair and let the wind take it. It took it far. "Journey takes us to new place. Land provides land. We must provide feet to walk it."

Jane raised an eyebrow. "Eh, I don't really know what that means."

"Maybe we'll meet again," Umna said. "This part of our path is over."

"I hope we meet again," Nox said, "and in better circumstances."

Oakley smiled. "You never know. There could be

such a thing as third chances."

"We sure could use folk like you all across the Wild North," Nox said. "Too many miles for just one sheriff. So, you know, maybe it ain't so bad that the path goes different ways. Maybe that's how we'll do the most good."

They said their parting words, exchanging hands and gifts.

Umna was the last to leave.

"How does it feel?" Nox asked her.

She looked at him silently.

"Justice, I mean."

"Good," she said. She stared off in the direction of Ilouayisca, where there was nothing now. "A little."

"It only ever helps a little."

"A little is a lot to those who have nothing else."

Nox nodded solemnly. She had no home now, no family. She was like him, like Oakley. See, you don't choose to become a drifter. Life chooses for you.

Umna gave Nox another pebble, this one with a different marking.

"My blessing to hunt," she said.

Nox didn't need it, but, like all the other little things, it helped.

They parted ways, and Nox rode on—yet this time it was he who looked back. He looked at the few folk who believed in him in times of trouble, even those he'd had that trouble with. He took a little comfort in the knowledge that, no matter how lonely it got out there in the wild, there were others just like him. Maybe they didn't all walk together—but they didn't walk alone.

Five went in as one then, like all five digits of a hand. But Nox was a lone wolf, so he vowed to fight on with just his two pistols for company. And he could do it, because, well, he was the finger on the trigger. He got to decide who lived or died. He was the Coilhunter. He was the law.

About the Author

Dean F. Wilson was born in Dublin, Ireland in 1987. He started writing at age 11, and has since become a *USA Today* and *Wall Street Journal* Bestselling Author.

He is the author of the *Children of Telm* epic fantasy trilogy, the *Great Iron War* steampunk series, the *Coilhunter Chronicles* science-fiction western series, the *Hibernian Hollows* urban fantasy series, and the *Infinite Stars* space opera series.

Dean previously worked as a journalist, primarily in the field of technology. He has written for *TechEye*, *Thinq*, *V3*, *VR-Zone*, *ITProPortal*, *TechRadar Pro*, and *The Inquirer*.

www.deanfwilson.com